DOTTY DIMPLE
AT PLAY

SOPHIE MAY

DOTTY DIMPLE AT PLAY.

CHAPTER I.

"THE BLIND-EYED CHILDREN."

"You is goin' off, Dotty Dimpwil."

"Yes, dear, and you must kiss me."

"No, not now; you isn't gone yet. You's goin' nex' day after this day."

Miss Dimple and Horace exchanged glances, for they had an important secret between them.

"Dotty, does you want to hear me crow like Bantie? 'Cause," added Katie, with a pitying glance at her cousin, "'cause you can't bear me bimeby, when you didn't be to my house."

"That will do, you blessed little Topknot," cried Horace, as the shrill crowing died on the air, and the pink bud of a mouth took its own shape again. "Now I just mean to tell you something nice, for you might as well know it and be happy a day longer: mother and you and I are going to Indianapolis to-morrow with Dotty—going in the cars."

"O!" exclaimed the child, whirling about like a leaf in a breeze. "Going to 'Naplis, yidin' in the cars! O my shole!"

"Yes, and you'll be good all day—won't you, darling, and not hide mamma's spools?"

"Yes, I won't if I don't 'member. We for salt, salt, salt," sang Flyaway (meaning mi, fa, sol). Then she ran to the bureau, perched herself before it on an ottoman, and talked to herself in the glass.

"Now you be good gell all day, Katie Clifford—not dishbey your mamma, not hide her freds o' spools, say fank you please. O my shole!"

So Katie was made happy for twenty-four hours.

"After we sleep one more time," said she, "then we shall go."

She wished to sleep that "one more time" with Dotty; but her little head was so full of the journey that she aroused her bedfellow in the middle of the night, calling out,—

"We's goin' to 'Naplis,—we for salt, salt, salt,—yidin' in the cars,

Dotty Dimpwil."

It was some time before Dotty could come out of dreamland, and understand what Katie said.

"Won't you please to hush?" she whispered faintly, and turned away her face, for the new moon was shining into her eyes.

"Let's we get up," cried Katie, shaking her by the shoulders; "don't you see the sun's all corned up bwight?"

"O, that's nothing but just the moon, Katie Clifford."

"O ho! is um the moon? Who cutted im in two?" said Flyaway, and dropped to sleep again.

Dotty was really sorry to leave aunt Maria's pleasant house, and the charming novelties of Out West.

"Phebe," said she, with a quiver in her voice, when she received the tomato pincushion, "I like you just as well as if you wasn't black. And, Katinka, I like you just as well as if you wasn't Dutch. You can cook better things than Norah, if your hair isn't so nice."

This speech pleased Katinka so much that she patted the letter O's on each side of her head with great satisfaction, and was very sorry she had not made some chocolate cakes for Dotty to eat in the cars.

Uncle Henry did not like to part with his bright little niece. She had been so docile and affectionate during her visit, that he began to think her very lovely, and to wonder he had ever supposed she had a wayward temper.

The ride to Indianapolis was a very pleasant one. Katie thought she had the care of the whole party, and her little face was full of anxiety.

"Don't you tubble yourself, mamma," said She; "I'll look out the winner, and tell you when we get there."

"Don't let her fall out, Horace," said Mrs. Clifford; "I have a headache, and you must watch her."

"Has you got a headache, mamma? I's solly. Lean 'gainst ME, mamma."

Horace wished the conductor had been in that car, so he could have seen Miss Flyaway trying to prop her mother's head against her own morsel of a shoulder—about as secure a resting-place as a piece of thistle-down.

"When was it be dinner-time?" said she at last, growing very tired of so much care, and beginning to think "'Naplis" was a long way off.

But they arrived there at last, and found Mr. Parlin waiting for them at the depot. After they had all been refreshed by a nice dinner, and Flyaway had caught a nap, which took her about as long as it takes a fly to eat his breakfast, then Mr. Parlin suggested that they should visit the Blind Asylum.

"Is it where they make blinds?" asked Dotty.

"O, no," replied Mr. Parlin; "it is a school where blind children are taught."

"What is they when they is blind, uncle Eddard?"

"They don't see, my dear."

Flyaway shut her eyes, just to give herself an idea of their condition, and ran against Horace, who saved her from falling.

"I was velly blind, then, Hollis," said she, "and that's what is it."

"I don't see," queried Dotty,—"I don't see how people that can't see can see to read; so what's the use to go to school?"

"They read by the sense of feeling; the letters are raised," said Mr.

Parlin. "But here we are at the Institute."

They were in the pleasantest part of the city, standing before some beautiful grounds which occupied an entire square, and were enclosed by an iron fence. In front of the building grew trees and shrubs, and on each side was a play-ground for the children.

"Why, that house has windows," cried Dotty. "I don't see what people want of windows when they can't see."

"Nor me needer," echoed Katie. "What um wants winners, can't see out of?"

They went up a flight of stone steps, and were met at the door by a blind waiting-girl, who ushered them into the visitors' parlor.

"Is she blind-eyed?" whispered Flyaway, gazing at her earnestly. "Her eyes isn't shut up; where is the see gone to?"

Mrs. Clifford sent up her card, and the superintendent, who knew her well, came down to meet her. He was also "blind-eyed," but the children did not suspect it. They were much interested in the specimens of bead-work which were to be seen In the show-cases. Mr. Parlin bought some flowers, baskets, and other toys, to carry home to Susy and Prudy. Horace said,—

"These beads are strung on wires, and it would be easy enough to do that with one's eyes shut; but it always did puzzle me to see how blind people can tell one color from another with the ends of their fingers."

The superintendent smiled.

"That would be strange indeed if it were true," said he; "but it is a mistake. The colors are put into separate boxes, and that is the way the children distinguish them."

"I suppose they are much happier for being busy," said Mr. Parlin. "It is a beautiful thing that they can be made useful."

"So it is," said the superintendent. "I am blind myself, and I know how necessary employment is to MY happiness."

The children looked up at the noble face of the speaker with surprise.

Was he blind?

"Why does he wear glasses, then?" whispered Dotty. "Grandma wears 'em because she can see a little, and wants to see more."

The superintendent was amused. As he could not see, Dotty had unconsciously supposed his hearing must be rather dull; but, on the contrary, it was very quick, and he had caught every word.

"I suppose, my child," remarked he, playfully, "these spectacles of mine may be called the gravestones for my dead eyes."

Dotty did not understand this; but she was very sorry she had spoken so loud.

After looking at the show-cases as long as they liked, the visitors went across the hall into the little ones' school-room. This was a very pleasant place, furnished with nice desks; and at one end were book-cases containing "blind books" with raised letters. Horace soon discovered that the Old Testament was in six volumes, each volume as large as a family Bible.

In this cheerful room were twenty or thirty boys and girls. They looked very much like other children, only they did not appear to notice that any one was entering, and scarcely turned their heads as the door softly opened.

Dotty had a great many new thoughts. These unfortunate little ones were very neatly dressed, yet they had never seen themselves in the glass; and how did they know whether their hair was rough or smooth, or parted in the middle? How could they tell when they dropped grease-spots on those nice clothes?

"I don't see," thought Dotty, "how they know when to go to bed! O, dear! I should get up in the night and think 'twas morning; only I should s'pose 'twas night all the whole time, and not any stars either! When my father spoke to me, I should think it was my mother, and say, 'Yes'm.' And p'rhaps I should think Prudy was a beggar-man with a wig on. And never saw a flower nor a tree! O, dear!"

While she was musing in this way, and gazing about her with eager eyes which saw everything, the children were reading aloud from their odd-looking books. It was strange to see their small fingers fly so rapidly over the pages. Horace said it was "a touching sight."

"I wonder," went on Dotty to herself, "if they should tease God very hard, would he let their eyes come again? No, I s'pose not."

Then she reflected further that perhaps they were glad to be blind; she hoped so. The teacher now called out a class in geography, and began to ask questions.

"What can you tell me about the inhabitants of Utah?" said she.

"I know," spoke up a little boy with black hair, and eyes which would have been bright if the lids had not shut them out of sight,—"I know; Utah is inhabited by a religious INSECT called Mormons."

The superintendent and visitors knew that he meant sect and they laughed at the mistake; all but Dotty and Flyaway, who did not consider it funny at all. Flyaway was seated in a chair, busily engaged in picking dirt out of the heels of her boots with a pin.

Horace was much interested in the atlases and globes, upon the surface of which the land rose up higher than the water, and the deserts were powdered with sand. These blind children could travel all about the world with their fingers as well as he could with eyes and a pointer.

The teacher—a kind-looking young lady—was quite pleased when Mr. Parlin said to her,—

"I see very little difference between this and the Portland schools for small children."

She wished, and so did the teachers in the other three divisions, to have the pupils almost forget they were blind.

She allowed them to sing and recite poetry for the entertainment of their visitors. Some of them had very sweet voices, and Mrs. Clifford listened with tears. Their singing recalled to her mind the memory of beautiful things, as music always does; and then she remembered that through their whole lives these children must grope in darkness. She felt more sorrowful for them than they felt for themselves. These dear little souls, who would never see the sun, were very happy, and some of them really supposed it was delightful to be blind.

Their teacher desired them to come forward, if they chose, and repeat sentences of their own composing. Some things they said were very odd. One bright little girl remarked very gravely,—

"Happy are the blind, for they see no ghosts."

This made her companions all laugh. "Yes, that's true," thought Dotty. "If people should come in here with ever so many pumpkins and candles inside, these blind children wouldn't know it; they couldn't be frightened. I wonder where they ever heard of ghosts. There must have been some naughty girl here, like Angeline."

CHAPTER II.

EMILY'S TRIALS.

At three o'clock the little blind girls all went out to play in one yard, and the little blind boys in the other.

"Goin' out to take their air," said Katie. Then she and Dotty followed the girls in respectful silence.

Almost every one had a particular friend; and it was wonderful to see how certain any two friends were to find one another by the sense of feeling, and walk off together, arm in arm. It was strange, too, that they could move so fast without hitting things and falling down.

"When I am blindfolded," thought Dotty, "it makes me dizzy, and I don't know where I am. When I think anything isn't there, the next I know I come against it, and make my nose bleed."

She was not aware that while the most of these children were blind, there were others who had a little glimmering of eyesight. The world was night to some of them; to others, twilight.

They did not know Dotty and Katie were following them, and they chatted away as if they were quite by themselves.

"Emily, have you seen my Lilly Viola?" said one little girl to another. "Miss Percival has dressed her all over new with a red dressing-gown and a black hat."

The speaker was a lovely little girl with curly hair; but her eyes were closed, and Dotty wondered what made her talk of "seeing" a doll.

Emily took "Lilly Viola," and travelled all over her hat and dress and kid boots with her fingers.

"Yes, Octavia," said she, "she is very pretty—ever so much prettier than my Victoria Josephine."

Then both the little girls talked sweet nothings to their rag babies, just like any other little girls.

"Is the dollies blind-eyed, too?" asked Katie, making a dash forward, and peeping into the cloth face of a baby.

The little mamma, whose name was Octavia, smiled, and taking Katie by the shoulders, began to touch her all over with her fingers.

"Dear little thing!" said she; "what soft hair!"

"Yes," replied Katie; "velly soft. Don't you wish, though, you could see my new dress? It's got little blue yoses all over it."

"I know your dress is pretty," said Octavia, gently, "and I know you are pretty, too, your voice is so sweet."

"Well, I eat canny," said Katie, "and that makes my voice sweet. I'se got 'most a hunnerd bushels o' canny to my house."

"Have you truly?" asked the children, gathering about Flyaway, and kissing her.

"Yes, and I'se got a sweet place in my neck, too; but my papa's kissed it all out o' me."

"Isn't she a darling?" said Octavia, with delight.

"Yes," answered Dotty, very glad to say a word to such remarkable children as these; "yes, she is a darling; and she has on a white dress with blue spots, and a hat trimmed with blue; and her hair is straw color. They call her Flyaway, because she can't keep still a minute."

"Yes, I does; I keeps still two, free, five, all the minutes," cried Katie; and to prove it, she flew across the yard, and began to pry into one of the play-houses.

"She doesn't mean to be naughty; you must scuse her," spoke up Dotty, very loud; for she still held unconsciously to the idea that blind people must have dull ears. "She is a nice baby; but I s'pose you don't know there are some play-houses in this yard, and she'll get into mischief if I don't watch her."

"Why, all these play-houses are ours," said little curly-haired Emily; "whose did you think they were?"

"Yours?" asked Dotty, in surprise; "can you play?"

Emily laughed merrily.

"Why not? Did you think we were sick?"

Dotty did not answer.

"I am Mrs. Holiday," added Emily; "that is, I generally am; but sometimes I'm Jane. Didn't you ever read Rollo on the Atlantic?"

Dotty, who could only stammer over the First Reader at her mother's knee, was obliged to confess that she had never made Rollo's acquaintance.

"We have books read to us," said Emily. "In the work-hour we go into the sitting-room, and there we sit with the bead-boxes in our laps, making baskets, and then our teacher reads to us out of a book, or tells us a story."

"That is very nice," said Dotty; "people don't read to me much."

"No, of course not, because you can see. People are kinder to blind children—didn't you know it? I'm glad I had my eyes put out, for if they hadn't been put out I shouldn't have come here."

"Where should you have gone, then?"

"I shouldn't have gone anywhere; I should just have staid at home."

"Don't you like to stay at home?"

Emily shrugged her shoulders.

"My paw killed a man."

"I don't know what a paw is," said Dotty.

"O, Flyaway Clifford, you've broken a teapot!"

"No matter," said Emily, kindly; "'twas made out of a gone-to-seed poppy.

Don't you know what a paw is? Why, it's a paw"

In spite of this clear explanation, Dotty did not understand any better than before.

"It was the man that married my maw, only maw died, and then there was another one, and she scolded and shook me."

"O, I s'pose you mean a father 'n mother; now I know."

"I want to tell you," pursued Emily, who loved to talk to strangers. "She didn't care if I was blind; she used to shake me just the same. And my paw had fits."

The other children, who had often heard this story, did not listen to it with great interest, but went on with their various plays, leaving Emily and Dotty standing together before Emily's baby-house.

"Yes, my paw had fits. I knew when they were coming, for I could smell them in the bottle."

"Fits in a bottle!"

"It was something he drank out of a bottle that made him have the fits.

You are so little that you couldn't understand. And then he was cross.

And once he killed a man; but he didn't go to."

"Then he was guilty," said Dotty, in a solemn tone. "Did they take him to the court-house and hang him?"

"No, of course they wouldn't hang him. They said it was the third degree, and they sent him to the State's Prison."

"O, is your father in the State's Prison?"

Dotty thought if her father were in such, a dreadful place, and she herself were blind, she should not wish to live; but here was Emily looking just as happy as anybody else. Indeed, the little girl was rather proud of being the daughter of such a wicked man. She had been pitied so much for her misfortunes that she had come to regard herself as quite a remarkable person. She could not see the horror in Dotty's face, but she could detect it in her voice; so she went on, well satisfied.

"There isn't any other little girl in this school that has had so much trouble as I have. A lady told me it was because God wanted to make a good woman of me, and that was why it was."

"Does it make people good to have trouble?" asked Dotty, trying to remember what dreadful trials had happened to herself. "Our house was burnt all up, and I felt dreadfully. I lost a tea-set, too, with gold rims. I didn't know I was any better for that."

"O, you see, it isn't very awful to have a house burnt up," said Emily; "not half so awful as it is to have your eyes put out."

"But then, Emily, I've been sick, and had the sore throat, and almost drowned—and—and—the whooping-cough when I was a baby."

"What is your name?" asked Emily; "and how old are you?"

"My name is Alice Parlin, and I am six years old."

"Why, I am nine; and see—your head! only comes under my chin."

"Of course it doesn't," replied Dotty, with some spirit. "I wouldn't be as tall as you are for anything, and me only six—going on seven."

"I suppose your paw is rich, and good to you, and you have everything you want—don't you, Alice?"

"No, my father isn't rich at all, Emily, and I don't have many things—no, indeed," replied Miss Dimple, with a desire to plume herself on her poverty and privations. "My aunt 'Ria has two girls, but we don't, only our Norah; and mother never lets me put any nightly-blue sirreup on my hangerjif 'cept Sundays. I think we're pretty poor."

Dotty meant all she said. She had now become a traveller; had seen a great many elegant things; and when she thought of her home in Portland, it seemed to her plainer and less attractive than it had ever seemed before.

"I don't know what you would think," said Emily, counting over her trials on her fingers as if they had been so many diamond rings, "if you didn't have anything to eat but brown bread and molasses. I guess you'd think that was pretty poor! And got the molasses all over your face, because you couldn't see to put it in your mouth. And had that woman shake you every time you spoke. And your paw in State's Prison because he killed a man. O, no," repeated she, with triumph, "there isn't any other little girl in this school that's had so much trouble as I have."

"No, I s'pose not," responded Dotty, giving up the attempt to compare trials with such a wretched being; "but then I may be blind, some time, too. P'rhaps a chicken will pick my eyes out. A cross hen flew right up and did so to a boy."

Emily paid no attention to this foolish remark.

"My paw writes me letters," said she. "Here is one in my pocket; would you like to read it?"

Dotty took the letter, which was badly written and worse spelled.

"Can you read it?" asked Emily, after Dotty had turned it over for some moments in silence.

"No, I cannot," replied Dotty, very much ashamed; "but I'm going to school by and by, and then I shall learn everything."

"O, no matter if you can't read it to me; my teacher has read it ever so many times. At the end of it, it says, 'Your unhappy and unfortunate paw.' That is what he always says at the end of all his letters; and he wants me to go to the prison to see him."

"Why, you couldn't see him."

"No," replied Emily, not understanding that Dotty referred to her blindness; "no, I couldn't see him. The superintendent Wouldn't let me go; he says it's no place for little girls."

"I shouldn't think it was," said Dotty, looking around for Flyaway, who was riding in a lady's chair made by two admiring little girls.

"There was one thing I didn't tell," said Emily, who felt obliged to pour her whole history into her new friend's ears; "I was sick last spring, and had a fever. If it had been scarlet fever I should have died; but it was imitation of scarlet fever, and I got well."

"I'm glad you got well," said Dotty, rather tired of Emily's troubles; "but don't you want to play with the other girls? I do."

"Yes; let us play Rollo on the Ocean," cried Octavia, who was Emily's bosom friend, and was seldom away from her long at a time, but had just now been devoting herself to Katie. "Here is the ship. All aboard!"

CHAPTER III.

PLAYING SHIP.

Now this ship was an old wagon-body, and had never been in water deeper than a mud puddle. A dozen little girls climbed in with great bustle and confusion, pretending they were walking a plank and climbing up some steps. After they were fairly on board they waved their handkerchiefs for a good by to their friends on shore. Then Octavia fired peas out of a little popgun twice, and this was meant as a long farewell to the land. Now they were fairly out on the ocean, and began to rock back and forth, as if tossed by a heavy sea.

"See how the waves rise!" said Emily, and threw up her hands with an undulating motion. "I can see them," she cried, an intent look coming into her closed eyes; "they are green, with white bubbles like soap suds. And the sun shines on them so! O, 'tis as beautiful as flowers!"

"Booful as flowers!" echoed Flyaway, who was one of the passengers; while

Dotty wondered how Octavia knew the difference between green and white.

She did not know; and what sort of a picture she painted in her mind of

the mysterious sea I am sure I cannot tell.

"Now," said Miriam Lake, the prettiest of the children, "it is time to strike the bells."

So she struck a tea-bell with a stick eight times.

"That is eight bells," explained she to Dotty, "and it means four o'clock. But, Jennie Holiday, where is the kitten? Why, we are not half ready."

The children never thought they could play "ship" without a kitten, a gray and white one which they put into a cage just as Jennie Holiday did, when she and Rollo travelled by themselves from New York to Liverpool. When the kitten had been brought, they had got as far as Long Island Sound, and they said the kitten was sent by a ship of war which had to be "spoken."

"This is a funny way to play," said Miriam. "Here we are at Halifax, and nobody has heaved the log yet."

"No," said Octavia; "so we can't tell how many knots an hour we are going."

"I'm going a great many knocks," cried Katie, whose exertions in rocking from side to side had thrown her overboard once.

"We never'll get to Liverpool in this world," said Emily, "unless Miss

Percival comes and steers the ship."

It happened at that very moment that Miss Percival came into the yard with aunt Maria.

"If you will excuse me, Mrs. Clifford," said she, laughing, "I will take command of this ship."

"No apologies are necessary," replied Mrs. Clifford. "I should be very glad to watch your proceedings. Is it possible, Miss Percival, that you are capable of guiding a vessel across the Atlantic?"

"I have often tried it," said Miss Percival, going on board; "but we sometimes have a shipwreck."

"Emily," said she, "you may heave the log." So Emily rose, and taking a large spool of crochet-cotton which Miss Percival gave her, held it above her head, turning it slowly, till a tatting shuttle, which was fastened at the end of the thread, fell to the ground. This was supposed to be the "log;" and Octavia, with one or two other girls, pretended to tug with much force in order to draw it in, for the ship was going so fast that the friction against the cord was very great. Knots had been made in the cotton, over which Emily ran her quick fingers.

"Ten knots an hour," said she.

"Very good speed," returned the captain. "I do not think we shall be able to take an observation to-day, as it is rather cloudy."

Sailors "take observations" at noon, if the sun is out, by means of a sextant, with which they measure the distance from the sun to the southern horizon. In this way the captain can tell the exact latitude of the ship; but Miss Percival made believe there was a storm coming up; so it was not possible to take an observation.

"It is two bells," said she: "the wind is out; there will be a fearful storm. I would advise the passengers to turn into their berths."

The children lay down upon the floor. "There, there," said Miriam Lake, who was playing Jennie Holiday; "my poor little kitty is just as seasick! Her head keeps going round and round."

"My head has did it too," chimed in Katie, rolling herself into a ball; "it keeps yocking yound and yound."

"I pitch about so in my berth," said Octavia, who was Rollo, "that next thing I shall be out on the floor. Hark! How the water is pouring in! I'm afraid the ship has sprung a leak; and if it has I must call the chambermaid."

Mrs. Clifford, who stood looking on, was quite amused at the idea of calling the chambermaid to stop a leak in the ship.

"Man the pumps!" said the captain. The girls tugged away at a pole in one end of the wagon, moving it up and down like a churn-dash.

"I do hope this wind will go down," sighed Emily.

"Well, it will," said simple Flyaway; "I hear it going."

"It is head wind and a heavy sea," remarked the captain; "but never fear; we shall weather the storm. We are now on the southern coast of Ireland. I don't think," added she, in a different tone, "it is best to be shipwrecked, children—do you? We will hurry into Liverpool, and then I think it likely your little visitors may enjoy keeping house with your dolls, or having a nice swing."

"I wish I could eat something," said Dotty, with a solemn face; "but I'm too sick."

"So'm I," groaned Flyaway. "I couldn't eat noffin'—'cept cake."

"If you are in such a condition as that," said the captain, "it is certainly high time we landed. And here comes a pilot boat with a signal flying. We will take the pilot on board," added she; drawing in another little girl. "And look! here we are now in Liverpool."

"We must go to the Adelphi," said Octavia; "that is where Rollo went, and found his father, and mother, and Thannie. But the kitten didn't ever get there—did it, Miss Percival?"

The voyage being ended, and with it the fearful seasickness, the children went to swinging, with their teacher to push them.

"Miss Percival," said aunt Maria, shaking hands with that excellent young lady, "I wish you joy of your noble employment. It is a blessed thing to be able to give so much pleasure to these dear little children."

"So it seems to me," replied Miss Percival. "They are always grateful, too, for every little kindness."

"They look very good and obedient," said Mrs. Clifford, in a low voice.

"So they are. Sometimes I think they are better than children who have eyes; perhaps because they cannot see to get into so much mischief," added Miss Percival, pinching Emily's cheek.

"Aunt 'Ria," said Dotty, in raptures, "don't they have good times here?"

"Yelly good times," said little Flyaway, clutching at her mother's dress.

"Mamma, I wish I was blind-eyed, too."

"You, my darling baby! Mother hopes that will never be. But if you cannot be blind-eyed yourself, perhaps you may make some of these little ones happy. Is there anything you would like to give away?"

Flyaway winked slowly, trying to think what she had at home that she no longer wished to keep.

"Yes, mamma," said she at last, with a smile of satisfaction, "I've got a old hat."

"O, fie, Katie! I dare say you would be very glad to part with that, for I remember you cried the other day when I asked you to wear it. Your old hat would not be a pretty present."

"Then I can't fink of noffin' else," said Katie, shaking her head; at the same time having a guilty recollection of several beautiful toys, and "'most a hunnerd bushels of canny;" that is to say, a small box of confectionery her uncle Edward had given her.

Mrs. Clifford had observed of late that her little daughter was not as generous as she could wish. Both Katie and Dotty were peculiarly liable to become selfish, as they were much petted at home, and had no younger brothers or sisters with whom to share their treasures. Mrs. Clifford did not insist upon Katie's making any sacrifice. The little one did not pity the blind children at all. They seemed so happy that she almost envied them. So did Miss Dimple. It was not, after all, very grievous to be blind, she thought, if one could live at this Institute and have such nice plays.

"Aunt 'Ria thinks I ought to give them something, I s'pose. When I get home I mean to ask mamma and grandma to dress a beautiful doll, and I'll send it to Emily. She'll keep it to remember me by; and it won't cost any of my money if papa buys the head."

"Good by, Emily," said she, as she parted from her. "I hope there won't any more bad things happen to you."

"But I s'pose there will," replied Emily, cheerfully.

Mr. Parlin and Horace were waiting in the hall, and the latter was impatiently watching the tall clock. They had been in the greenhouse, looking at the flowers, and in the shop, where the blind boys learn to make brooms and brushes.

"Well, ladies, are you ready to go?" asked Mr. Parlin, taking Flyaway by the hand.

"Yes, we ladies is ready," replied she. So this was the end of their visit at the Institute.

After they had gone away, the little blind girls said to one another,—

"What nice children those are! Which is the prettiest, Alice or Katie?"

For they always spoke of people and things exactly as if they could see them.

CHAPTER IV.

A SPOILED DINNER.

Next morning, Dotty Dimple and her father started for Maine. Flyaway did not like this at all. Her cousin had been so pleasant and so entertaining that she wished to keep her always.

"What for you can't stay, Dotty Dimpwil?"

"O," said Dotty, tearing herself away from the little clinging arms, "I must go home and get ready for Christmas."

"No, you musser," persisted Katie; "we've got a Santa Claw in our chimley; you musser go home."

"It isn't for Santa Claus at all, darling it is for my papa and mamma's wedding. To stand up, so they can be married over again. Now kiss me, and let me go."

"Her's goin' home to Kismus pie," remarked Katie, as she took her mournful way with her mamma to the house where they were visiting. She did not know what a wedding might be, but was sure it had pies in it.

"There goes a right smart little girl," said Horace, with a sweep of his thumb towards the Cleveland cars. "If it wasn't for Prudy, I should like her better than any other cousin I have in the world."

"She is an engaging child," replied his mother, "and really seems to be outgrowing her naughty ways."

Thus, you see, Dotty Dimple, in coming away from Indiana, had left in the minds of her friends only "golden opinions." Perhaps she was rather overrated. Everything had gone well with her during her visit; why should she not be pleasant and happy? I am inclined to think there was the same old naughtiness in her heart, only just now it was asleep. We shall see.

Nothing remarkable occurred on the homeward journey, except that Mr. Parlin bought some gold-fishes in Boston, and carried them home as a present to Mrs. Read. They travelled one night in a sleeping-car, and by that means reached Portland a day earlier than they were expected.

Dotty hardly knew whether to be glad or sorry for this. There was a great deal to be said on both sides of the question. She had anticipated the pleasure of being met at the depot by Susy and Prudy, and now that was not to be thought of; but it would be delightful to give the family a surprise. On the whole, she was very well satisfied.

As they drove up to the new home, however, what was their astonishment to find it closed! There was not even a window open, or any other sign that the house was inhabited. Dotty ran to every door, and shook it.

"Why, papa, papa, do you s'pose there's anybody dead?"

"The probability is, Alice, that they have gone away. I will run over to Mrs. Prosser's, and see if she knows anything about it."

Mrs. Prosser was the nearest neighbor on the left. Her little daughter came to the door in tears, having hurt herself against a trunk in the hall.

"Miss Carrie," said Mr. Parlin, "can you tell me where Mrs. Parlin and the rest of the family are gone?"

"Yes, Caddy Prosser, the house is shut up," added Dotty, "and I'm afraid they're dead."

"I don't know where they're gone, nor anything," sobbed Carrie. "I didn't know the trunk was in the entry, and I came so fast I fell right over it."

"I am very sorry you are hurt," said Mr. Parlin. "Is your mother at home?"

"No, sir, she isn't; her trunk came, but she didn't."

There was no information to be obtained at the Prossers'; so Mr. Parlin went to Mr. Lawrence's, the nearest neighbor on the right, making the same inquiries; but all he learned was, that a carriage had been seen standing at Mr. Parlin's door; who had gone away in it nobody could tell.

Dotty paced the pavement with restless steps, her mind agitated by a thousand wild fancies: Grandma Read never went anywhere; perhaps she was locked up in the house, and Zip too. Norah was at Cape Elizabeth; she had walked out to see her friend Bridget, the girl with red hair; and, just as likely as not, she didn't ever mean to come back again. Mother, and Susy, and Prudy had gone to Willowbrook, to grandpa Parlin's—of course they had,—and left grandma Bead all alone in the house, with nothing to eat. How strange! How unkind!

"Grandma!" she called out under Mrs. Read's window.

There was no answer. Dotty fancied the white curtain moved just a little; but that was because a fly was balancing himself on its folds. Grandma was not there, or, if she was, she must be very sound asleep. O, dear, dear! And here were Dotty and her father come home a day earlier than they were expected; and instead of giving the family a joyful surprise, they had a surprise themselves, only not a joyful one, by any means. How impolite it was in everybody, how unkind, to go away! At first, Dotty had been alarmed; but now her indignation got the better of her fears. When she did see Prudy again,—the sister who pretended to love her so much,—she wouldn't take the presents out of her trunk for ever so long, just to tease the naughty girl!

Meanwhile her father did not appear to be at all disturbed.

"Perhaps they have gone to the Islands, or somewhere else not far away, to spend the day. It is now nearly two o'clock. You may go to the Preble House with me, and take-your dinner, and then I will unlock the house, and find some one to stay with you till night. Would you like that? Or would you prefer to go at once to your aunt Eastman's? You may have your choice."

Dotty reflected about half a minute. "I will go to aunt Eastman's, if you please, papa."

This appeared to her decidedly the most dignified course. She would go to aunt Eastman's, and she would not be in the least haste about coming back again. She would teach her sisters, especially Prudy, that it is best to be hospitable towards one's friends when they have been away on a long journey. Her anger may seem very absurd; but you must remember, little friends, that Dotty Dimple had now become a travelled young lady; she had seen the world, and her self-esteem had grown every day she had been away. Her heart was all aglow with love towards the dear ones at home, and it was very chilling to find the door locked in her face. She did not stop to reflect that no unkindness had been intended.

As they drove to aunt Eastman's, her father observed that her bright little face was very downcast, but supposed her sadness arose from the disappointment. There are depths of foolishness in children's hearts which even their parents cannot fathom.

Strange to say, neither Mr. Parlin nor Dotty had thought that the family might be visiting at Mr. Eastman's; but such was the case. It was Johnny's birthday, and his father had sent the carriage into the city that morning for Mrs. Parlin, grandma Read, and the children. As for Norah, Dotty was right with regard to her; she had walked out to the Cape to see the auburn-haired Bridget.

"I'm glad Johnny was born to-day instead of to-morrow," said Prudy, "for to-morrow we wouldn't go out of the house for anything, auntie."

"I can seem to see cousin Dimple," said Percy; "she'll carry her head higher than ever."

Prudy cast upon the youth as strong a look of disapproval as her gentle face could express.

"Percy, you mustn't talk so about Dotty. She is my sister. She isn't so very proud; but if I was as handsome as she is, I should be proud too."

"O, no; she is very meek—Dimple is; just like a little lamb. Don't you remember that verse she used to repeat?—

'But, chillens, you should never let

  Your naughty ankles rise;

19

Your little hands were never made

  To tear each uzzer's eyes—out.'"

"If she's cross, it's because you and Johnny tease her so," said Prudy.

"I think it's a shame."

Percy only laughed. He and Prudy were sitting in the doorway, arranging bouquets for the dinner-table. Susy joined them, bearing in her hands some dahlias and tuberoses.

"Why, Prudy," said she, "what makes your face all aflame?"

"She has been fighting for your little dove of a sister," replied Percy; "the one that went West to finish her education."

This speech only deepened the color in Prudy's face, though she tried hard to subdue her anger, and closed her lips with the firm resolve not to open them again till she could speak pleasantly.

"Look!" exclaimed Percy; "there's a carriage turning the corner. Why, it's Dimple herself and uncle Edward!"

"It can't be!"

"It is!"

Both little girls ran to the gate.

"O, father! O, Dotty! Why, when did you get home?"

By this time Mrs. Parlin had come out: also Mrs. Eastman and Johnny.

Everybody was as surprised and delighted as possible; and even Miss

Dimple, sitting in state in the coach, was perfectly satisfied, and

condescended to alight, instead of riding through the carriage gateway.

"O, Dotty Dimple, I'm so glad to see you!" cried Prudy.

"It is my sister Alice,

And she is grown so dear, so dear,

That I would be the jewel

That trembles at her ear,—

only you don't wear ear-rings, you know."

"Are you glad to see me, though, Prudy? Then what made you go off and shut the house up?"

"O, we didn't expect you till to-morrow; and it's Johnny's birthday.

Dinner is almost ready; aren't you glad? Such a dinner, too!"

"Any bill of fare?" asked Dotty, with a sudden recollection of past grandeur.

"A bill of fare? O, no; those are for hotels. But there's almost everything else. Now you can go up stairs with me, and wash your face."

Dotty appeared at table with smooth hair and a fresh ruffle which Prudy had basted in the neck of her dress. She looked very neat and prim, and, as Percy had predicted, carried her head higher than ever.

"I suppose," said aunt Eastman, "you will have a great many wonderful things to tell us, Dotty, for I am sure you travelled with your eyes open."

"Yes'm; I hardly ever went to sleep in the cars. But when you said 'eyes,' auntie, it made me think of the blind children. We went to the 'Sylum to see them."

"How do they look?" asked Johnny.

"They don't look at all; they are blind."

"Astonishing! I'd open my eyes if I were they."

"Why, Percy, they are blind—stone-blind!"

"How is that? How blind is a stone?"

Dotty busied herself with her turkey. Her Eastman cousins all had a way of rendering her very uncomfortable. They made remarks which were intended to be witty, but were only pert. They were not really kind-hearted, or they would have been more thoughtful of the feelings of others.

"Alice," said dear Mrs. Read, trying to turn the conversation, "I see thee wears a very pretty ring."

Dotty took it off her finger, and passed it around for inspection.

"I never had a ring before," said she, with animation. "I never had anything to wear—'cept clothes"

Percy laughed.

"I found the pearl in an oyster stew, grandma. It is such a very funny place Out West"

"Yes, it is really a pearl," said Percy, "only spoiled by boiling. Look her, Toddlekins; oysters don't grow Out West; they grow here on the coast. You'd better study astronomy."

Dotty took refuge in silence again, like an oyster withdrawing into his shell.

"O, Dotty," said Susy, presently, "tell me what you saw Out West. I want to hear all about it."

"Well, I saw a pandrammer," replied Dotty, briefly.

"What in the world is that?" said Johnny.

"It is a long picture, and they keep pulling it out like India rubber."

"She means a panorama" cried Johnny. "Why, I went to one last night. We can see as much as you can, without going Out West, either."

Here was another sensation. Dotty might as well have been eating ashes as the delirious dinner before her.

"Don't you like your pudding, dear?" asked aunt Eastman.

"O, yes'm; I always like coker-whacker" replied the unfortunate Dotty, stumbling over the word tapioca.

In spite of their mother's warning frown, the three young Eastmans laughed, while Susy and Prudy, who had kinder hearts and better manners, drew down their mouths with the greatest solemnity.

"I ain't going to speak another word," cried the persecuted little traveller, setting down her goblet, and hitting it against her plate till it rang again.

"Error!" called out Florence from the other side of the table; "there's no such word as ain't."

This was too much. Dotty had smarted under these cruel blows long enough.

She hastily arose from the table, and rushed out of the room.

"Florence and Percy, you are both very thoughtless," said Mrs. Eastman, reprovingly.

Mrs. Parlin looked deeply pained, as she always did when her little daughter gave way to her temper; but she made no allusion to the subject, and tried to go on with her dinner as if nothing had happened.

Dotty ran into the front yard, threw herself on the ground, and buried her face in a verbena bed.

There! it wasn't of any use; she couldn't be good; it wouldn't last! When she had just come home, and had so many things to tell, and supposed everybody would be glad to see her and hear her talk,—why, Percy and Florence must just spoil it all by laughing. O, it was too bad!

"I wish I hadn't come! I wish I'd been switched off!" sighed Dotty, meaning, if she meant anything, that she wished the cars had whirled her away to the ends of the earth, instead of bringing her home, where people were all ready with one accord to trample her into the dust.

"Here I've been 'way off, and know how to travel, and keep my ticket in my glove. Six years old, going on seven. Been down in a coal mine,—Prudy never'd dare to. Had a jigger cut out of my side. Been to the 'Sylum. One of the conductors said, 'That's a fine little daughter of yours, sir.' I heard him. Aunt 'Ria washed all those grease-spots out of my dress, and I had on a clean ruffle. And then, just 'cause I couldn't say coker-whacker—"

"There, there, don't feel so bad, you precious sister," said a soothing voice; and a soft cheek was pressed to Dotty's, and a pair of loving arms clasped her close. "Percy was real too-bad, and so was Flossy—so there!"

"O, Prudy, I wish they were every one of 'em in the penitential, locked in, and Johnny too! Me just got home, and never did a single thing to them! And there they laughed right in my face!"

"But you know, dear, they don't think," said Prudy, who found it unsafe to sympathize too much with her angry sister; "they never do think; they don't mean any harm."

"I'll make 'em think!" cried Dotty, fiercely. "I'll scare 'em so they'll think! I'll take a pumpkin, and I'll take a watermelon, and I'll take—"

"Dear me, Dotty, that is a beautiful ring on your finger. I wish I had one just like it."

Dotty cast a suspicious glance at her sister.

"Don't you try to pacify ME, Prudy Parlin."

Prudy held a handful of southernwood to her nose, and smiled behind it.

"This isn't temper, Prudy Parlin, 'cause you said your own self they 'bused me."

"Such a cunning little pearl!" remarked Prudy, still admiring the ring; "how glad I should be if you'd wish it on to my finger, Dotty!"

"They 'bused me, Prudy Parlin, and you know it."

"Only till night, Dotty Dimple. Just wish it on till night."

"Well, there," exclaimed Dotty, at last; "hold out your finger if you can't stop teasing. But I haven't any temper, and you needn't act just's if you's trying to pacify me."

"O, thank you, Dotty; on my third finger."

"Now I've wished it on, Prudy; and its a good-enough wish for you, when you won't pity me; but now I'm going up in the bathing-room to stay, and you can't make me come down—not a single step."

"I shan't want you to come down, Dotty. There's the very place I'm going to myself. We'll carry up the needle-gun; it's the nicest thing to play with. Come, let's hurry up stairs the back way, little sister, for they'll be out from dinner, and see us."

Dotty needed no second hint. In half an hour she was so far recovered from the megrims as to be hungry; when Prudy secretly begged some pudding for her of the willing Angeline.

Then the same little peacemaker went to her cousins, and made them each and all promise to be more careful of her sister's feelings; after which there was nut-cracking in the wood-shed, and a loud call for Miss Dimple, who consented to go down after much urging, and was the merriest one of the whole party.

CHAPTER V.

PLAYING TRUANT.

For several days after her return Dotty Dimple was in a state of jubilee. She had a great deal to tell, and the whole household was ready to listen. Norah would stand with a dish or a rolling-pin in her hand, and almost forget what she had intended to do in her desire to hear every word Miss Dotty was saying.

Once, when she related her adventure with the pigeon-pie, grandma Read, who was clear-starching her caps, let the starch boil over on the stove; and at another time Mrs. Parlin was so much absorbed in a description of Phebe, that she almost spiced a custard with cayenne pepper.

All these evidences of interest were very flattering to Dotty. Sometimes she took Prudy one side, and told her the same story twice over, to which Prudy always listened with unfailing politeness. As I said before, while this excitement lasted Miss Dimple was in a state of jubilee. But by and by the novelty wore off; she had told the family everything she could possibly think of, and now longed for a few pairs of fresh ears into which to pour her stories. Everybody else was working for Christmas; Dotty alone was idle; for no one had time to give her a daily stint, and see that she accomplished it.

"After the holidays I shall have to go to school; so now is my time to play," said she to herself, "and I ought to play every minute, as tight as I can spring."

But she tried so hard to be happy that the effort was really very tiresome. If she had only had something to do, I am almost sure she would not have fallen into the misfortune which I am about to record.

One day her mother sent her to a worsted store to pattern some worsteds. A girl behind the counter gave her the right shades, and she slowly started for home. It was about four o'clock of a November day. Dotty, glancing idly at the sky, saw that the sun was already getting low.

"How queer it is!" thought she; "it seems as if the sun grows sleepy very early nowadays, and goes to bed right in the middle of the afternoon. Well, I declare, if there isn't Lina Rosenberg!"

The beautiful little Jewess was just turning an opposite corner, and, as usual, the sight of her face bewitched Dotty in a minute.

"O, Lina Rosenberg, come over here! How do you do?"

"I'm very well, Dotty: how do YOU do? Only I wish you wouldn't call me a BUG!"

"Well, then, Lina, you mustn't have bugs in your name if you don't want to be called by 'em. Did you know I'd been Out West?"

"No; you haven't, Dotty Dimple!"

"Yes, I have; you may ask my father. I kept my own ticket right in my glove, and took 'most the whole care of myself. Went to the Blind 'Sylum; found a pearl in an oyster; been 'way down in a coal mine; and—and—"

"Come to my house, won't you, and tell me all about it?" said Lina Rosenberg, looking as beguiling as possible, and taking Dotty's unresisting hand.

Dotty knew very well that her mother would never allow her to go to

Lina's house; but she did not like to say that, and she only replied,—

"I've matched my worsteds, and now I must go home."

"O, you can go home afterwards. My mother said to me to-day, 'Do you bring Dotty Dimple home to supper this very night. She'll be so glad to see you!'"

Dotty gave another glance at the sky, then one at the city clock.

"What time do you drink tea, Lina?"

"At five, 'most always."

Dotty had long felt a great curiosity about the domestic affairs of the Jews; and here was an unexpected opportunity to sit down at the very table with them. She had an invitation from the head of the family, and that was something which did not happen every day. She could go home any time afterwards; for their own tea-hour was not till half past six.

"I'll walk along with you a little way, Lina, and think it over."

It was true Mrs. Parlin did not approve of Mandoline or any of her family; but Dotty thought she would forget that, just for once.

"O, dear! I keep thinking how my mamma said, 'I do not wish you to play with Lina Rosenberg!' Now I can 'most always forget easy enough; but when I TRY to forget, it says itself over and over—and I remember just as hard!"

As they turned another corner they met Susy, who had been sent to the dye-house.

"Why, Dotty," said she, "what are you doing on that street?"

Lina spoke up very boldly,—

"She's going to the doctor's with me, Susy Parlin, to get a plaster for my mother."

At this wicked speech Dotty's heart almost sank into her boots; for she had never known before that Lina would tell a deliberate lie.

Lina lived in a little grocery store. Her father was gone away to-day,> and her mother had just served a customer with a pound of damp brown sugar, saying, as she clipped the string,—

"It's very cheap sweetening at that price; we are going to rise on it to-morrow."

After that she stood a minute in front of the store, and shook her head at Jacob, a little boy, some three years old, who was trying to balance a patent washboard against a tree which grew out of the brick pavement. It was a large, scrawny tree, which looked as if it was obliged to live there, but didn't want to, and had tried in vain to get burnt up in the Portland fire. From the lower branches of the tree depended a couple of dun-colored hams, and a painted board, with the words, "Good Family Butter."

"Come in, Jacob, you naughty boy!" said Mrs. Rosenberg, this time shaking him, because she was afraid he would injure the patent wash-board. Then Jacob, who had been waiting for the shaking, and would not stir without it, went in at the side door crying; for the family lived in one end of the store.

Mrs. Rosenberg had a great many children, and was obliged to work very hard at various employments. Just now she went to spreading pumpkin-seeds to dry under the stove. She was not expecting company; and when Mandoline entered with Dotty, she looked up from her work with a frown.

"Who've you brought home with you this time, Mandoline Rosenberg?" said she. "Take off your hat and hang it over them tommatuses; but mind yer don't drop it into that dish of lard."

"Mother," pleaded Mandoline, "we want to go up chamber to see my pretty things; her mother sent her a-purpose."

"No, she didn't; no such a thing! You're a master hand to pick up children and fetch 'em home here, and then crawl out of it by lying! Besides, you've got to knit. I must have those socks done by to-morrow noon, Mandy, or I'll know the reason why."

As Mrs. Rosenberg spoke, she pushed a waiter full of seeds under the stove as if she hated the very sight of them; and when she stood up again, Dotty observed that her dirty calico dress did not come anywhere near the tops of her calf-skin shoes.

"But, mother," said Mandoline, with a winning smile, "this is Dotty

Dimple, the little girl that gave me the needle-book."

This was partly true. Dotty had given Mandoline an old needle-book; but it had been in return for some maple sugar, which the little Jewess had pilfered from her father's store.

"Dotty Dimple, is it?" said Mrs. Rosenberg, with a sharp look at the little guest.

"I don't know now any better than I did before. That's a name for a doll-baby; I should say."

"Alice Parlin, mother."

"Is it? O, well; you may take her up stairs out of my way; but mind, you must knit every minute you're gone."

Dotty was greatly abashed by this reception, and would have rushed out of the house, but Mandoline held her fast.

"You shan't go a step," said she, "I'll hide your hat."

So Dotty, under peril of going home bareheaded, was obliged to creep up the rickety staircase with Mandoline. She likened her feelings on the occasion to those of a person whom "the mayor is putting in the lockup." Indeed, the "lock-up" was Dotty's dream of all the horrors, and she had no doubt it was the mayor himself who always stood with his hands outstretched, ready to thrust wicked people into it.

The chamber which the little girls entered was an unfinished one, and from the rafters hung paper bags of dried herbs; for, besides being a housekeeper and clerk, Mrs. Rosenberg was something of a doctress withal, and made "bitters" for her particular friends.

"Sit down here on the bed, Dotty Dimple, and look at my paper dolls," said Lina, producing from under a disjointed chair, an old cigar box full of paper heroes and heroines. Mandoline was an artist in he! way, and these figures were clad in the most brilliant costumes of silver and gold. Dotty was dazzled. Never before had it been her lot to see such magnificent dolls,— dolls which shone so in the sun; every one of them a king or a queen, and fit to wear a crown.

"O, Lina," sighed she, in ecstasy, "where do you get your silver and gold?"

"Tease for it," replied the little Jewess.

Dotty knew, to her own sorrow, that Lina was capable of teasing. It was hard to keep so much as an apple or a peppermint away from her if she happened to set her heart on it.

"I'll give you twenty dolls," said Lina, "if you'll let me have your ring; and it isn't a very pretty ring, either; looks like brass."

Dotty locked her fingers together.

"You can't tease away my owny dony pearl, Lina, if it is brass; so you needn't try."

"Mandoline!" called out Mrs. Rosenberg's sharp voice from down stairs, "are you at work?"

"O, dear!" said Lina, sauntering along to an old chest, and taking her knitting from the top of it; "that's always the way. I thought if you came, mother'd let me play."

Dotty understood from this remark why Lina had asked her to go home with her. It was not because she wished to hear any of Dotty's brilliant stories, for she had not asked a single question about Out West; it was because she hoped for a reprieve from the dreaded knitting.

"She's a real naughty little girl," thought Miss Dimple; "and if she hadn't hided my hat, I'd go right home."

There was a heavy tread on the stairs. Mrs. Rosenberg was coming up, partly to see if her daughter was knitting, and partly to hang a paper bag on the long pole overhead. Mandoline was dreadfully afraid of her mother, and, in her eagerness to be found hard at work, she rattled her needles very fast, while her fingers wandered aimlessly about among the stitches. Mrs. Rosenberg detected the cheat at once; and, as she was needing the money for the socks, she scolded Mandoline soundly, and pelted her pretty little hands, rat, tat, tat, with a steel thimble.

Dotty was a little startled, and peeped out at Lina from the corners of her eyes. Mrs. Rosenberg scolded so hard that the paper bags overhead seemed to rattle, and some yellow pollen dropped out of one of them like shooting stars.

Dotty had never known that there are such cruel people in the world; but let me tell you, little reader, every mother is not like the gentle, low-voiced woman who takes you in her lap, and kindly reproves you when you have done wrong. No; there are very different mothers; hard-working, ignorant ones, who do not know how to treat their children any more than you know how to build a brick house.

Mrs. Rosenberg was so severe and unreasonable, that her little daughter, through fear of her, had learned to deceive. Still Mrs. Rosenberg loved Mandoline, and would have been a better mother, perhaps, if she had only known how, and had not had so much work to do.

Presently she went down stairs, and left the little girls together.

"Good!" said Lina, in a low voice. "She's gone; now we'll play."

"But you can't knit if you play, Lina. Tell me where you hided my hat, 'cause I want to go home."

"You shan't go home till after supper, you little darling Dotty Dimple."

"O, but I must go, for my mother doesn't know where I am," said Dotty, in a dreary tone. She had no longer any curiosity regarding Jewish suppers; all she wanted was the liberty to get away. But it is always easier to fall into a trap than to get out of it. Mandoline would not produce the missing hat, and it was no light matter for Dotty to go down stairs, among the noisy, quarrelsome children, and beg the severe Mrs. Rosenberg to take her part. If she did so, perhaps the woman would pelt her with the steel thimble. Perhaps, too, she would say Mandoline might keep the hat. So Dotty played "synagogue," and all the while the sun was dropping down, down the sky, as if it had a leaden weight attached to it, to make it go faster.

CHAPTER VI.

A STRANGE VISIT.

The same warfare of words continued to come up from the kitchen, and presently the odor of sausages stole up, too; Mrs. Rosenberg was preparing supper. It seemed to the impatient Dotty that she was a long while about it; but she worked as fast as she could, with so many children clinging to her skirts, and impeding her movements.

"Supper, Mandoline!" called she at last, in a shrill voice; and the little girls went down.

The supper was palatable enough, but very unwholesome, and the table-cloth was dirty and wrinkled.

"You don't seem to like my cooking," said Mrs. Rosenberg, with a displeased glance at Dotty's full plate.

"Yes'm," replied the little guest, faintly; "but I've eaten up my appetite."

At the same time she swallowed a little oily gravy in desperation, and looked slyly to see if Solly was watching her. Yes, he was, and so were all the rest of the family, as if she had been a peculiar kind of animal, just caught and caged.

"I suppose they are dreadful nice folks at your house," continued Mrs. Rosenberg. "I almost wonder your mother let you come here to play with my poor little girl. Mandy's just as good as you are, though,—you can tell her so,—and she's got a sight prettier eyes."

Dotty's heart kept swelling and swelling, till presently it seemed as if there wasn't room enough in her whole body to hold it. She thought of the cheerful, orderly tea-table at home; she recalled her mother's gentle ways, her lovely face, and longed to kiss her cheek, and whisper, "Forgive me."

"Mamma'll be just as patient with me," thought Dotty; "she always is! But if I once get home, I'll never make her patient any more. I'll never run away again; not unless she asks me to—I won't."

The children, as fast as they finished their suppers, jumped up and ran away from the table—all but Solly, who had some faint idea that it was not polite to do so before company. He was a natural gentleman; and it was unfortunate that just at this time his mother was obliged to send him to Munjoy of an errand. Otherwise he would have made his sister give up Dotty's hat, and perhaps would have walked home with the unhappy child himself.

As it was, Dotty did not seem to have a friend in the world. It was now so dark that she hardly dared look out of doors; but even in the brightest daylight she could not have found her way home.

"You've got to stay all night," said Mandoline. "Isn't that splendid?"

Mandoline did not mean to be cruel. She had observed that her mother urged her own guests to stay, and sometimes kept them almost by force. This she supposed was true politeness. More than that, she was anxious, for private reasons, to hold Dotty, so she might not have to knit so much. She knew, too, that her mother was proud to have such a well-bred little girl in the house. So she would not give up Dotty's hat.

At eight o'clock, Dotty went to bed with Mandoline in the unfinished chamber, sorely against her will; and Mandoline told her such dreadful stories that she could not close her eyes for fright.

"This is the queerest house I was ever in," thought she, "and the queerest bed. I s'pose it's made of pin-feathers, for they stick into me awfully."

The bed was on the floor, and was founded upon woolsacks and buffalo skins. The sleeping arrangements in this house were somewhat peculiar. Mrs. Rosenberg was like the old woman in the shoe, and she stowed her numerous family away for the night in as little space as possible. For instance, the four youngest children slept together in one trundle-bed, two at the top and two at the bottom, their feet coming together in the middle. But Mandoline had left the trundle bed, and was lying on the floor with her guest. The companion the trundle-bed—little Kosina—was quite indignant at being deserted, and made a loud outcry, in the hope of attracting her mother's attention.

"I don't want to sleep alone!" said she; "I don't want to sleep alo-o-one!"

At another time Dotty would have laughed heartily. It was so absurd for a child to be lonesome when there were three in the bed! But Dotty was too low-spirited even to smile. Mrs. Rosenberg came up and boxed Rosina's ears; and after that the trundle-bed subsided.

At last, when Dotty supposed it must be midnight, though it was only nine o'clock, there came a loud knocking at the side door. She hid her face under the coverlet, feeling sure it was either a wild Indian or a highway robber.

"Don't be afraid," said Mandoline, rousing herself. "It is somebody after beer, and mother has locked up the store."

No, it was Mr. Parlin's voice which spoke. Dotty's swollen heart gave a great bound, and then sank heavier than ever.

"My little daughter Alice has run away." That was what he said. "Is she in your house, Mrs. Rosenberg?"

"Yes," replied Mrs. Rosenberg, "I expect its likely she is; but she and my Mandoline's been abed and asleep two hours."

"O, papa, I'm wide awake!" cried little Dotty, with an eager shriek, which pierced the rafters.

"Good night, then," said Mr. Parlin, coldly.

"O, but, papa, I want to go home. What did my mamma say about me?"

"She said she had sent you of an errand. When you have finished your errand, you may come home. Good night."

"O, NOT good night!" screamed Dotty, almost falling down stairs in her haste, and fastening her dress as she ran. "It was 'cause Lina hid my hat; and that was why—"

"By the way," said Mr. Parlin, without paying the slightest attention to his half-frantic little daughter, who was clinging to his knees, and pleading with her whole soul, "Mrs. Rosenberg, I'm sorry to trouble you, but if you will be kind enough to keep this little runaway girl till I send for her, I shall be very much obliged."

"O, certainly, Mr. Parlin; certainly, sir," replied the Jewess, smiling very sweetly, and trying to pat Dotty's head, which was in such violent motion that she only succeeded in touching the end of her nose. No one who had looked at Mrs. Rosenberg at that moment would have suspected her of being a vixen. She was sure Mr. Parlin would pay her handsomely if she kept his daughter there for a day or two; and the prospect of a little money always made the poor woman very amiable.

"Thank you, madam," said Mr. Parlin, gently disengaging himself from Dotty. "When you are tired of my little daughter, will you please let me know? Goodnight, Mrs. Rosenberg; good-night, Alice."

And, before Dotty had time to scream again, he was gone.

For a moment she stood quite still, gazing at the door-latch; then rushed out into the darkness, calling, "Papa, papa!" But Mrs. Rosenberg laid her strong hands upon her, and brought her back.

"So your mother didn't say you might come? I thought it was queer. Hush! hush! Don't go into fits, child. There are no bears in this house, and nothing will hurt you."

Mrs. Rosenberg's manner was much kinder than it had been before; and with a child's quick insight, Dotty perceived that her father's coming had wrought the change.

"I want to go home! I want to go home!" cried she, with another passionate outburst. "O, take me—do! They won't send for me, never! Take me, and I'll give you—O, Mrs. Rosenberg, I'll give you—"

For a little while there was quite a scene at the little grocery, and it repented Mandoline that she had ever hidden Dotty's hat. The trundle-bed waked up at both ends and screamed; the black and tan dog, who slept under the counter in the store, barked lustily; the parrot in the blue cage called out, "Quit that! quit that!" and Mrs. Rosenberg was afraid a policeman would come in to inquire the cause of the uproar. She pattered about in a pair of her husband's cotton-velvet slippers, and tucked all her little ones into bed again, very much as if they had been clothes in a boiler, which she was forcing down with a stick. She was a woman who would be obeyed; and Dotty, finding it of no use to hold out against fate, went up stairs at last, and lay down beside Mandoline on the "pin-feathers."

This stolen visit had turned out quite, quite different from her anticipations. Instead of a delightful supper of some mysterious Jewish cookery, she had been drinking gall and wormwood. That Lina would not let her go—THAT was the gall; that her father made her stay—THIS was the wormwood.

"She is a tough piece," sighed Mrs. Rosenberg, as she laid her weary limbs to repose; "I didn't know, one while, but she'd get away in spite of me. I wonder what her father'll pay me. He seems to think this is a house of correction. Her mother won't be likely to let her stay more than one day. I'll have on the best table-cloth for breakfast; and along in the forenoon I'll fetch out some macaroni cakes and lager beer; that'll coax her up, I guess."

Just then Mrs. Rosenberg down stairs and Dotty Dimple up stairs both fell asleep. One dreamed of running away and being chased by a dog with a hat on his head, who barked "Good-night" as fiercely as a bite. The other dreamed of money and brown sugar. And all the while the rats were treating themselves to nibbles of wood; but nobody heard them. Be careful, old rats! Your teeth have done mischief before now! The night wore on to the wee small hours, when a loud noise like a cannon startled Mrs. Rosenberg; or was she dreaming? The house was shaken to its very foundation, as if by an earthquake, and the room was full of smoke. She was just running for the children, when the building fell together with a crash, the roof was blown off into the street, the windows were shivered to atoms, and tongues of flame leaped madly up from the ruins.

What did it mean? She was so stunned by the shock that she scarcely cared whether one of her children was spared or not; she only thought in her stupor that Mr. Parlin would not pay her for Dotty's lodging if the child was blown to pieces.

"I know how it happened," said she, twitching at her own hair to arouse herself. "Just as Abraham always said; the rats have been nibbling matches in the store; they've burned a hole through the floor, and set fire to that keg of gunpowder. Yes, that's it!"

CHAPTER VII

PLAYING PRISONER.

I know how it happened, too. It came of eating sausages. Mrs. Rosenberg, after she was fairly awake, felt so uncomfortable and oppressed that she went up stairs to see if the children were safe. Really, I do suppose those little human souls were precious to her, after all.

There lay Mandoline and Dotty side by side on the buffalo skins; and the Jewish mother stood in her short night-dress, with a tallow candle in her hand, and gazed at them tenderly. That horrible dream had stirred the fountain of love in her heart They made a beautiful picture, and there was no stain of evil in their young faces. It seems as if the angel of Sleep flies away with loads of naughtiness, for he always leaves sleeping children looking very innocent. But, alas! he brings back next morning all he carried away, for the little ones wake up with just as bad hearts as ever.

"What sweet little creeters!" said Mrs. Rosenberg, bending over and kissing them both; "just like seraphims right out of the clouds."

Softly, madam! If a drop of tallow should fall on them from that candle, they might take to themselves wings and fly away. That was what Cupid did in the fairy story, and you are in fairy-land yourself, Mrs. Rosenberg; you are still half asleep.

She looked at Mandoline's perfect little hand, lying outside the patchwork quilt.

"It doesn't seem, now," murmured the mother, with a tear in her eye, "that I could ever whack them pretty fingers with a thimble. I do believe if I wasn't pestered to death with everything under the sun to do, I might be kind o' half-way decent."

Perhaps the poor woman told the truth; I think she did.

Then, as she stood there, she breathed a little prayer without any words,— not for herself—for she did not suppose God would hear that,—but for her children that she "banged about" every day of their lives.

She was not really a Jewess, for she had no religion of any sort, and never went to church; but I am sure of one thing: little overworked Mandoline would have loved her mother better if she had known she ever prayed for her at all.

In the morning, Mrs. Rosenberg was just as hard and sharp as ever; she could not stop to be pleasant. Dotty longed to get away; but she was an exile from her own dear home; whither could she turn?

It was a cold morning, and the children ran down stairs half dressed and shivering. Dotty spread out her stiff, red fingers before the cooking-stove like the sticks of a fan. "O, hum!" thought she, drearily, "I wish I could see the red coals in our grate. My mamma wouldn't let me go to the table with such hair as this. Prudy'd say 'twas 'harum scarum.' But I can't brush it with a tooth-comb, 'thout any glass—so there!"

Dotty's curly hair looked quite as respectable as Mandoline's. Mrs. Rosenberg was far too busy to attend to her children's heads. They might be rough on the outside, and full of mischief inside; but she could not stop to inquire.

"What a dreadful nice breakfast!" remarked Judith, rubbing her hands, and accidentally hitting little Jacob, who forthwith spilled some molasses on the clean table-cloth, and had his ears boxed in consequence. It was very evident that this meal was a much better one than usual—a sort of festival in honor of Dotty Dimple: Dutch cheese and pickles, mince-pie and gingerbread, pepper-boxes and green and yellow dishes, were mixed up together as if they had been stirred about with a spoon.

Dotty had not intended to eat a mouthful; but after her light supper of the night before, she was really hungry, and, in spite of her best resolves, the fish-hash and corncake gradually disappeared from her plate.

After breakfast she felt more resigned, and armed herself to meet her fate. Mrs. Rosenberg graciously allowed Mandoline to lay aside her tedious knitting, and give her undivided attention to her guest. Dotty had no heart for play.

"Seems as if I should choke in this house," said she; "let's go out and breathe."

The air inside the house was rather stifling from a mixture of odors, and soon the grocery began to fill with loud-talking men and boys; but not the least of Dotty's troubles was the black and tan dog, who seemed to have just such a temper as Mrs. Rosenberg, and would certainly have scolded if he had had the gift of speech.

The two little girls went out to walk; but it was not a pleasant street where the grocery stood, and Dotty hurried on to a better part of the town. They fluttered about for two or three hours, as aimless as a couple of white butterflies. Just as they were turning to go back to the dismal little grocery, which Dotty thought was more like a lock-up than ever, they met Mr. and Mrs. Parlin riding out in a carriage.

Dotty felt a sudden tumult of joy and shame, but the joy was uppermost. She rushed headlong across the street, swinging her arms and startling the horse, who supposed she was some new and improved kind of windmill, dressed up in a little girl's clothes.

"O, my darling mamma, my darling mamma!"

To her surprise, the horse did not stop. He only pricked up his ears, and looked with displeasure at the windmill, but kept along as before.

"Mamma, mamma, I say!"

Her mother never even looked at her, but turned her gaze to the blackened trees, the heaps of ruin along the pavement.

"O; papa! O, stop, papa! It's me! It's Dotty!"

Mr. Parlin bent on his runaway daughter a glance of indifference, and called out, in passing,—

"What strange little girl is this, who seems to know us so well? It looks like my daughter Alice. If it is, she needn't come to my house to-day; she may go and finish her visit at Mrs. Rosenberg's."

Then the horse trotted on,—indeed, he had never paused a moment,—and carried both those dear, dear people out of sight.

What did they mean? What had happened to Dotty Dimple, that her own father and mother did not know her?

She looked down at the skirt of her dress, at her gaiters, at her little bare hands, to make sure no wicked fairy had changed her. Not that she suspected any such thing. She understood but too well what her father and mother meant. They knew her, but had not chosen to recognize her, because they were displeased.

Dotty's little heart, the swelling of which had net gone down at all during the night, now ached terribly. She covered her face with her hands, and groaned aloud.

"Don't," said Mandoline, touched with pity. "They no business to treat you so."

"O, Lina, don't you talk! You don't know anything about it. You never had such a father'n mother's they are! And now they won't let me come into the house!"

This wail of despair would have melted Mrs. Parlin if she could have heard it. It was only because she thought it necessary to be severe that she had consented to do as her husband advised, and turn coldly away from her dear little daughter. Dotty was a loving child, in spite of her disobedience, and this treatment was almost more than she could bear. She found no consolation in talking with Lina, for she knew Lina could not understand her feelings.

"She hasn't any Susy and Prudy at her house, nor no anything" thought Dotty. "If I lived with Mrs. Rosenberg and that dog, I'd want to be locked out; I'd ask if I couldn't. But, O, my darling mamma! I've been naughty too many times! When I'd been naughty fifty, sixty, five hundred times, then she forgave me; but now she can't forgive me any more; it isn't possible."

Dotty staggered against a girl who was drawing a baby-carriage, but recovered herself.

"It isn't possible to forgive me any more. She told me not to go on the water, and I went. She told me not to have temper, and I had it. Every single thing she's told me not to do, I always went and did it. She said, 'I do not wish you to play with Lina Rosenberg;' and then I went right off and played with her. I didn't have a bit good time; but that's nothing. She hided my hat—Lina did; but if I'd gone home, straight home, and not gone to her house, then she couldn't have hided it.

"I was naughty; I was real naughty; I was as naughty as King Herod and King Pharaoh. Nobody'll ever love me. I'm a poor orphanless child! I've got a father'n mother, but it's just the same as if I didn't, for they won't let me call 'em by it. O, they didn't die, but they won't be any father'n mother to ME!

"'What strange little girl is this?' that's what my papa said. ' Looks like my daughter Alice!' O, I wish I could die!"

"Come, come," said Lina; "let's go home. Mother said you and I might have some macaroni cakes and lager beer, if we wouldn't let the rest of 'em see us at it."

"I don't care anything about your locker beer, Lina Rosenberg, nor your whiskey and tobacco pipes, either. Nor neither, nor nothing," added the desolate child, standing "stock still," with the back of her head against a pile of bricks, her eyes closed, and her hands folded across her bosom.

"There, there; you're a pretty sight now, Dotty Dimple! What if you should freeze so! Come along and behave."

"I can't, I can't!"

"If you don't, Dotty, I'll have to go into that barber's shop. I know the man, and I'll make him carry you home piggerback"

"Well, if I've got to go, I'll go," said Dotty, rousing herself, and starting; "but I'd rather be dead, over'n over; and wish I was; so there!"

CHAPTER VIII.

PLAYING THIEF.

This day was the longest one to be found in the almanac; it was longer than all the line of railroad from Maine to Indiana and back again.

Dotty shut her lips together, and suffered in silence. But when the afternoon was half spent, it suddenly occurred to her that if she did not go home she should die. Soldiers had died of homesickness, for she had heard her father say so. She had not been able to swallow a mouthful of dinner, and that fact was of itself rather alarming.

"Perhaps I'm going to have the typo. Any way, my head aches. Besides, my papa didn't say I mustn't go home. He said I must finish my visit, and I have. O, I've finished that all up, ever and ever and ever so long ago."

She and Mandoline went out again to "breathe," Mrs. Rosenberg giving her daughter a warning glance from the doorway, which meant, "Be watchful, Mandy!" for the look of fixed despair on the little prisoner's face gave the woman some anxiety lest she should try to escape.

The unhappy child walked on in silence, twisting a lock of her front hair, and looking up at the sky. A few soft snow-flakes were dropping out of the clouds. Every flake seemed to fall on her heart. Winter was coming. It was a gray, miserable world, and she was left out in the cold. She remembered she had been happy once, but that was ages ago. It wasn't likely she should ever smile again; and as for laughter, she knew that was over with her forever. Susy and Prudy were at home, making book-marks and cologne mats; they could smile, for they hadn't run away.

"I shouldn't think my mamma'd care if I went in at the back door," thought Dotty, meekly. "If she locks me out, I can lie down on the steps and freeze."

But the question was, how to get away from Mandoline, who had her in charge like a sharp-eyed sheriff.

"That's the street I turn to go to my house—isn't it, Lina?" asked she, quickly.

"I shan't tell you, Dotty Dimple. Why do you ask?"

"'Cause I'm going home. I'm sick. Good by."

"But you musn't go a step, Dotty Dimple."

"Yes, I shall; you're not my mamma, Lina Rosenberg; you mustn't tell me what to do."

"Well, I'm going everywhere you go, Dotty, but I shan't say whether it's the way to your house, or the way to Boston; and you don't know."

Dotty was not to be so easily baffled.

"I don't know myself, Lina Rosenberg, but if you're so mean as not to tell, I can ask somebody else that will tell—don't you see?"

This was a difficulty which Lina had not provided for. She was very sorry Dotty had come out "to breathe."

Very soon they overtook a lady, who pointed out the right street to Dotty; and it was in an opposite direction from the one she was taking.

"Now I've found out, Miss Rosenberg, and you can't help yourself."

"Well, I shall go with you, Dotty, just the same. I shall go right up to your house, and tell your mother you've run away again"

It was very disagreeable to Miss Dimple to be pursued in this way; but she put on an air of defiance.

"I shouldn't think you'd want to go where you wasn't wanted, Miss Rosenberg."

Lina had never intended to do such a thing; she had not courage enough.

"O, dear! what shall I do to make you go back with me? My mother'll scold me awfully for letting you get away."

"Well, there; you've got the dreadfulest mother, Lina, and I'm real sorry; but it's no use to tease me; I wouldn't go back, not if you should cut me up into little pieces as big as a cent."

Lina was ready to fall upon her knees, right on the pavement. She offered Dotty paper dolls enough to people a colony; but Miss Dimple was as firm as a rock, now her face was once set towards home. Lina turned on her heel, and slowly walked away. Dotty called after her:—

"There, Lina, now you've told an awful story! You said you'd go to my house, and tell my mother I'd run away again; and now you don't dare go; so you've told an awful wicked story."

With this parting thrust at her tormentor, Dotty turned again to the misery of her own thoughts. Her home was already in sight; but the uncertainty as to her reception there made her little feet falter in their course. Her head sank lower and lower, till her chin snuggled into the hollow of her neck, and her eyes peered out keenly from under her hat, to make sure no one was watching. There was a door-yard on one side of the house. She touched the gate-latch as gently as if it had been a loaded gun, and crept noiselessly along to the side door. Here she paused. Her heart throbbed loudly; but, in spite of that, she could hear Norah walking about, and rattling the covers of the stove, as she put in coal.

Dotty's courage failed. What if Norah should make believe she didn't know her, and shut the door in her face?

"I can't see Norah, and hear her say, 'What strange little girl is this? It looks like our Alice; but it can't be any such a child!' No, I can't see anybody. I've finished my visit; I have a right to come home; but p'rhaps they won't think so. I feel's if I wasn't half so good as tea-grounds, or coffee-grounds, or potato-skins," continued she, with a pang of despair. "I know what I'll do; I'll go down cellar; that's where the rats stay; and if I am bad, I hope I'm as good as a rat, for I don't bite."

One of the cellar windows had been left out in order to admit coal. Through this window crept Dotty, regardless of her white stockings and crimson dress. When she had fairly got her head through the opening, and was no longer afraid of being seen, she breathed more freely.

"Here I am! Not a bit of me out. But I must go on my tipsy-toes, or they'll hear me, and think it's a buggler"

There was quite a steep hill to walk over, and she found it anything but a path of roses. Once or twice she stumbled and fell upon her hands and knees.

"Seems to me," said she, drawing out her foot, which had sunk above the ankle in coal,—"seems to me I have as many feet as a caterpillar."

But she kept on, down the Hill of Difficulty, till she reached solid ground. It was not a very cheerful apartment, that is certain. The light had much difficulty in getting in at the little windows, and when it did fight its way through it was not good for much; it was a gloomy light, and looked as if it had had a hard time.

Dotty went up to the furnace for comfort. It was a tall, black thing, doing its best to give warmth and cheer to the rooms up stairs, but it was of no use to the cellar. It was like some brilliant people, who shine in society, but are dull and stupid at home. Dotty opened the furnace door, and tried to warm her cold fingers.

"Why, my hands are as black as a sip," sighed she; as if she could have expected anything else.

There did not seem to be one ray of hope in her little dark soul. She had no tears to shed,—she seldom had,—but when she was in trouble, she was always in the lowest depths.

"Pretty well for me to make believe I was a thief, and was going to steal! 'Who is this strange little girl?' said he; 'it looks like—'"

She heard voices near the cellar door. What if Norah should come down after butter? Dotty was not prepared for that. She could not hide in the keg of lard, of course; and what should she do?

"My head is tipside up; I can't think." Then she began to wonder how long she could live down there, in case she was not discovered.

"I s'pose I can climb up on the swing shelf, and sleep there nights. I can hide behind things in the daytime, and when I'm hungry I can eat out of the jars and boxes."

The sound of voices came down distinctly from the kitchen overhead. Dotty crouched behind an apple barrel, and listened. Grandma Read was talking to Mrs. Parlin, who seemed to be in another room.

"Mary, my glasses are gone this time," said she. "If little Alice were only here, I should set her to hunting."

"She don't know I'm in the house this minute," thought Dotty; "no, under the house. Dear me!"

With that she walked softly up the stairs, and listened at the door-latch; for the sound of her grandmother's voice was encouraging, and Dotty, in her loneliness, longed to be near the dear people of the family, even if she could not see them.

"Edward," said her mother,—what music there was in her voice!—"if you are going after that dear child, you'd better take a shawl to wrap her in, for it is snowing fast. And be sure to tell her we love her dearly, every one of us, and don't believe she will ever run away again."

"O, was her papa going after her? Did they love her, after all? Were they willing to keep her in the house?"

Dotty opened the door before she knew it. "O, mamma, mamma!" cried she, rushing into her mother's arms.

"Why, Dotty, you darling child, where did you come from?" exclaimed Mrs. Parlin, in great surprise, kissing the little, dirty girl, and taking her right to her heart, in spite of the coal-dust.

"If you'll let me stay at home," gasped Dotty, "if you'll let me stay at home, I'll live in the kitchen, and won't go near the table."

"Where did you come from?" said Mr. Parlin, kissing a clean place on

Dotty's black face, and laughing under his breath.

"I came through the cellar window, papa."

"Through the cellar window, child?"

"Yes, papa; I didn't s'pose you'd care!"

"Care! My dear, your mother is the one to care! Just look at your stockings!"

"There was coal there, thrown in," said Dotty, with a quivering lip; "and I had to walk over it, and under it, and through it."

"Was my little daughter afraid to come in by the door?"

"I didn't know's you wanted me, papa.

"I thought you'd say, 'What strange child is this?'"

Mr. Parlin, looking at the black streaks on Dotty's woeful face, found it very difficult to keep from laughing. "A strange child' she appeared to be, certainly.

"But I'd got my visit all finished up, ever and ever so long ago."

"So you really chose to come back to us, my dear?"

"O, papa, you don't know! Did you think, did you s'pose—"

Here Dotty broke down completely, and, seizing her father's shirt-bosom in both her grimy hands, she buried her face in it, and sprinkled it with tears of ink.

There was great surprise throughout the house when Dotty's arrival became known.

"We didn't know how to live without you any longer," said Prudy; "and tomorrow Thanksgiving Day."

"But I never should have come up," said Dotty, "if I hadn't heard mamma talk about loving me just the same; I never could have come up."

"Excuse me for smiling," said Prudy; "but you look as if you had fallen into the inkstand. It is so funny!"

Dotty was not at all amused herself; but after she was dressed in clean clothes, she felt very happy, and enjoyed her supper remarkably well. The thought that they "didn't know how to live without her" gave a relish to every mouthful.

It was a delightful evening to the little wanderer. The parlor looked so cheerful in the rosy firelight that Dotty thought she "would like to kiss every single thing in the room." It was unpleasant out of doors, and the wind blew as if all the people in the world were deaf, and must be made to hear; but Dotty did not mind that. She looked out of the window, and said to Prudy,—

"Seems as if the wind had blown out all the stars; but no matter—is it?

It is all nice in the house."

Then she dropped the curtain, and went to sit in her mother's lap. Not a word of reproach had been uttered by any one yet; for it was thought the child had suffered enough.

"Mamma," said Dotty, laying her tired head on her mother's bosom, "don't you think I'm like the prodigal's—daughter? Yesterday I felt a whisper 'way down in my mind,—I didn't hear it, but I felt it,—and it said, 'You mustn't disobey your mamma; you mustn't play with Lina Rosenberg!'"

"Only think, my child, if you had only paid attention to that whisper!"

"Yes, mamma, but I tried to forget it, and by and by I did forget it—almost. There's one thing I know," added Dotty, clasping her hands together; "I'll never run away again. If I'm going to, I'll catch myself by the shoulder, and hold on just as hard!"

"My blessed child, I hope so," said Mrs. Parfin, with tears in her eyes and a stronger faith in her heart than she had felt for many a day that Dotty really meant to do better. "You don't know how it did distress your papa and me to have you stay in that house a night and a day; but we hoped it would prove a lesson to you; we meant it for your best good."

To make sure the lesson would not be forgotten, Prudy read her little sister a private lecture. She had written it that afternoon with carmine ink, on the nicest of tinted paper. Dotty received it very humbly, and laid it away in the rosewood box with her precious things.

PRUDY'S LECTURE.

"We must keep good company, Dotty, or not any at all. This is a fact.

"Even an apple is known by the company it keeps. Grandpa Parlin says if you put apples in a potato bin, they won't taste like apples—they'll taste like potatoes.

"Sometimes I think, Dotty, you'd be as good and nice as a summer-sweeting, if you wouldn't play with naughty children, like Lina Rosenberg; but if you do, you'll be like a potato, as true as you live.

"Finis."

CHAPTER IX

THANKSGIVING DAY.

The next day was Thanksgiving. Dotty wakened in such a happy mood that it seemed to her the world had never looked so bright before.

"I don't think, Prudy, it's the turkey and plum pudding we're going to have that makes me so happy—do you?"

"What is it, then, little sister?"

"O, it's 'cause I dreamed I was sleeping on pin-feathers, and woke up and found I wasn't. You'd feel a great deal better, Prudy, if you'd run away and had such a dreadful time, and got home again."

"I don't want to try it," returned Prudy, with a smile.

"No; but it's so nice to be forgiven!" said Dotty, laying her hand on her heart, "it makes you feel so easy right in here."

A fear came over Prudy that the little runaway had not been punished enough. But Dotty went on:—

"It makes you feel as if you'd never be naughty again. Now, if my mamma was always thumping me with a thimble, and scolding me so as to shake the house, I shouldn't care; but when she is just like an angel, and forgives me, I do care."

"I'm so glad, Dotty! I think, honestly, mother's the best woman that ever lived."

"Then why didn't she marry the best man?" asked Dotty, quickly.

"Who is that?"

"Why, Abraham Lincoln, of course." Prudy laughed.

"Yes; I suppose Mr. Lincoln was the best man that ever lived; but papa comes next."

"Yes," said Dotty; "I think he does. And I'd rather have him for a father than Mr. Lincoln, 'cause I'm better 'quainted with him. I shouldn't dare kiss the President. And, besides that, he's dead."

"You're a funny girl, Dotty; but what you say is true. Everything happens just right in this world."

"Does it?" said Dotty, wrinkling her brows anxiously; "does it, now truly?"

"Yes, indeed, Dotty. Anybody wouldn't think so, but it does."

"Then I suppose it happens right for me to be a bad girl and run away."

"No, indeed, Dotty; because you can help it. Everything is right that we can't help; that's what I mean."

"Then I s'pose 'twas right for me to crawl through the cellar window," said Dotty; "for I'm sure I couldn't help it"

"O, dear me! you ask such queer questions that I can't answer them, Dotty Dimple. All I know is this: everything happens just right in this world—when you can't help it."

With which sage remark Prudy stepped out of bed, and began to dress herself. Dotty planted her elbow in the pillow, and leaned her head on her hand.

"I don't believe it happens just right for Mrs. Rosenberg to keep that dog, or to thump so with a thimble; but, then, I don't know."

"I'm hurrying to get dressed," said Prudy. "The first bell has rung."

"Why, I never heard it," cried Dotty, springing up. "I wouldn't be late to-day for anything."

Prudy looked anxiously at her little sister to see if she was cross; but her face was as serene as the cloudless sky; she had waked up right, and meant to be good all day. When Dotty had one of her especially good days, Prudy's cup of happiness was full. She ran down stairs singing,—

"Thank God for pleasant weather!

Shout it merrily, ye hills,

And clap your hands together,

Ye exulting little rills.

"Thank him, bird and birdling,

As ye grow and sing;

Mingle in thanksgiving,

Every living thing,

Every living thing,

Every living thing."

Dotty was so anxious to redeem her character in everybody's eyes, that she hardly knew what she was doing. Mrs. Parlin sent her into the kitchen with a message to Norah concerning the turkey; but she forgot it on the way, and stood by Norah's elbow gazing at the raisins, fruit, and other nice things in a maze.

"What did my mamma send me here for? She ought to said it over twice. Any way, Norah, now I think of it, I wish you please wouldn't starch my aprons on the inside; starch 'em on the outside, 'cause they rub against my neck."

"Go back and see what your mamma wants," said Norah, laughing.

"Why, mamma," cried Dotty reappearing in the parlor quite crestfallen—" why, mamma, I went right up to Norah to ask her, and asked her something else. My head spins dreadfully."

Mrs. Parlin repeated the message; and Dotty delivered it this time correctly, adding,—

"Now, Norah, I'm all dressed for dinner; so I can do something for you just as well as not. Such days as, this, when you have so much to do, you ought to let me help."

To Dotty's surprise Norah found this suggestion rather amusing.

"For mercy's sake," said she, "I have got my hands full now; and when you are round, Miss Dotty, and have one of your good fits, it seems as if I should fly."

"What do you mean by a good fit?"

"Why, you have spells, child—you know you do—when butter wouldn't melt in your mouth."

"Do I?" said Dotty. "I thought butter always melted in anybody's mouth.

Does it make my mouth cold to be good, d'ye s'pose?"

"La, me, I don't know," replied the girl, washing a potato vigorously.

"I might wash those potatoes," said Dotty, plucking Norah's sleeve; "do you put soap on them?"

"Not much soap—no."

"Well, then, Norah, you shouldn't put any soap on them; that's why I asked; for my mother just washes and rinses 'em; that's the proper way."

"For pity's sake," said Norah, giving the little busybody a good-natured push. "What's going on in the parlor, Miss Dotty? You'd better run and see. If you should go in there and look out of the window, perhaps a monkey would come along with an organ."

"No, he wouldn't, Norah, and if he did, Prudy'd let me know."

As Dotty spoke she was employed in slicing an onion, while the tears ran down her cheeks; but a scream from Norah caused her to drop the knife.

"Why, what is it?" said Dotty.

"Ugh! It's some horrid little animil crawling down my neck."

"Let me get him," cried Dotty, seizing a pin, and rushing at poor Norah, who tried in vain to ward off the pin and at the same time catch the spider.

"Will you let me alone, child?"

"No, no; I want the bug myself," cried Dotty, pricking Norah on the cheek.

"Want the bug?"

"Yes; mayn't I stick him through with a pin from ear to ear? I know a lady Out West that's making a c'lection of bugs."

"Well, here he is, then; and a pretty scrape I've had catching him; thanks be to you all the same, Miss Dimple."

As it turned out to be only a hair-pin, Dotty shook her head in disdain, and went on slicing onions.

"Sure now," said Norah, "I should think you'd be wanting to go and see what's become of your sister Prudy. Maybe she's off on the street somewhere, and never asked you to go with her."

"Now you're telling a hint," exclaimed Dotty, making a dash at a turnip. "I know what you mean by your monkeys and things; you want to get me away. It's not polite to tell hints, Norah; my mamma says so."

But as Dotty began to see that she really was not wanted, she concluded to go, though she must have it seem that she went of her own accord, and not because of Norah's "hints."

"Did you think it was a buggler, when I opened the cellar-door last night, Norah?"

"No; I can't say as I did—not when I looked at you," replied

Norah, gravely.

"'Cause I'm going into the parlor to ask mother if she thought I was a buggler. I believe I won't help you any more now, Norah; p'rhaps I'll come out by and by."

So Dotty skipped away; but it never occurred to her that she had been troublesome. She merely thought it very strange Norah did not appreciate her services.

"I s'pose she knows mother'll help her if I don't," said she to herself.

Dotty's goodness ran on with a ceaseless flow till two o'clock, when that event took place which the children regarded as the most important one of the day—that is, dinner.

After the silent blessing, Mr. Parlin turned to his youngest daughter, and said,—

"Alice, do you know what Thanksgiving Day is for?"

"Yes, sir; for turkey."

"Is that all?"

"No, sir; for plum pudding."

"What do you think about it, Prudy?"

"I think the same as Dotty does, sir," replied Prudy, with a wistful glance at her father's right hand, which held the carving knife.

"What do you say, Susy?"

"It comes in the almanac, just like Christmas, sir; and it's something about the Pilgrim Fathers and the Mayflower."

"No, Susy; it does not come in the almanac; the Governor appoints it. We have so many blessings that he sets apart one day in the year in which we are to think them over, and be thankful for them."

"Yes, sir; yes, indeed," said Susy. "I always knew that."

"Now, before I carve the turkey, what if I ask the question all around what we feel most thankful for to-day? We will begin with grandmamma."

"If thee asks me first," said grandma Read, clasping her blue-veined, beautiful old hands, "I shall say I have everything to be thankful for; but I am most thankful for peace. Thee knows how I feel about war."

The children thought this a strange answer. They had almost forgotten there had ever been a war.

"Now, Mary, what have you to say?" asked Mr. Parlin of his wife.

"I am thankful we are all alive," replied Mrs. Parlin, looking at the faces around the table with a loving smile.

"And I," said her husband, "am thankful we all have our eyesight. I have thought more about it since I have visited two or three Blind Asylums. Susy, it is your turn."

"Papa, I'm thankful I'm so near thirteen."

Mr. Parlin stroked his mustache to hide a smile. He thought that was a very young remark.

"And you, Prudy?"

"I'm so thankful, sir," answered Prudy, reflecting a while, "so thankful this house isn't burnt up."

"Bless your little grateful heart," said her father, leaning towards her and stroking her cheek. "For my part, I think one fire is quite enough for one family. I confess I never should have dreamed of being thankful we hadn't had two. Well, Alice, what have you to say? I see a thought in your eyes."

"Why, papa," said Dotty, laying her forefingers together with emphasis,

"I've known what I'm thankful for, for two days. I'm thankful Mrs.

Rosenberg isn't my mother!"

A smile went around the table.

"But, papa, I am, truly. What should I want her for a mother for?"

"Indeed, I see no reason, my child, since you already have a pretty good mother of your own."

"Pretty good, papa!" said Dotty, in a tone of mild reproof. "Why, if she was YOUR mother, you'd think she was very good."

"Granted," returned Mr. Parlin.

"I don't think you'd like it, papa, to have her scold so she shakes down cobwebs."

"Who?"

"Mrs. Rosenberg."

"Never mind, my dear; we will not discuss that woman to-day. I hope you will some time learn to pronounce her name."

Then followed a few remarks from Mr. Parlin upon our duty to the Giver of all good things; after which he began at last to carve the turkey. The children thought it was certainly time he did so. They were afraid their thankfulness would die out if they did not have something to eat pretty soon.

CHAPTER X.

GRANDMA'S OLD TIMES.

Grandma Read was in her own room, sitting before a bright "clean" fire. She did not like coal; she said it made too much dust; so she always used wood. She sat with her knitting in her hands, clicking the needles merrily while she looked into the coals.

People can see a great many things in coals. Just now she saw the face of her dear husband, who had long ago been buried out of her sight. He had a broad-brimmed hat on his head, and there was a twinkle in his eye, for he had been a funny man, and very fond of a joke. Grandma smiled as if she could almost hear him tell one of his droll stories.

Presently there was a little tap at the door. Grandma roused herself, and looked up to see who was coming.

"Walk in," said she; "walk in, my dear."

"Yes'm, we came a-purpose to walk in," replied a cheery voice; and Prudy and Dotty danced into the room, with their arms about each other's waists.

"O, how pleasant it seems in here!" said Prudy; "when I come in I always feel just like singing."

"Thee likes my clean fire," said grandma.

"But, grandma," said Dotty, "I should think you'd be lonesome 'thout anybody but you."

"No, my dear; the room is always full."

"Full, grandma?"

"Yes; full of memories."

The children looked about; but they only two sunny windows; a table with books on it, and a pair of gold fishes; a bed with snowy coverlet and very high pillows; a green and white carpet; a mahogany bureau and washing-stand; and then the bright fireplace, with a marble mantel, and a pair of gilt bellows hanging on a brass nail.

It was a very neat and cheerful room; but they could not understand why there should be any more memories in it than there were in any other part of the house.

"We old people live very much in the past," said grandma Read. "Prudence, if thee'll pick up this stitch for me, I will tell thee what I was thinking of when thee and Alice came in."

So saying, she held out the little red mitten she was knitting, and at the same time took the spectacles off her nose and offered them to Prudy. Prudy laughed.

"Why, grandma! my eyes are as good as can be. I don't wear glasses."

"So thee doesn't, child, surely. I am a little absent-minded, thinking of old mother Knowles."

"Grandma, please wait a minute," said Prudy, after she had picked up the stitch. "If you are going to tell a story, I want to get my work and bring it in here. I'm in a hurry about that scarf for mamma."

"It is nothing very remarkable," said Mrs. Read, as the children seated themselves, one on each side of her, Prudy with her crocheting of violet and white worsted, and Dotty with nothing at all to do but play with the tongs.

"Mrs. Knowles was a very large, fleshy woman, who lived near my father's house when I was a little girl. Some people were very much afraid of her, and thought her a witch. Her sister's husband, Mr. Palmer, got very angry with her, and declared she bewitched his cattle."

"Did she, grandma?" asked Dotty.

"No, indeed, my dear; and couldn't have done it if she had tried."

"Then 'twas very unpertinent for him to say so!"

"He was a lazy man, and did not take proper care of his animals. Sometimes he came over and talked with my mother about his trials with his wicked sister-in-law. He said he often went to the barn in the morning, and found his poor cattle had walked up to the top of the scaffold; and how could they do that unless they were bewitched?"

"Did they truly do it? I know what the scaffold is; it is a high place where you look for hen's eggs."

"Yes; I believe the cows did really walk up there; but this was the way it happened, Alice: They were not properly fastened into their stalls, and being very hungry, they went into the barn for something to eat. The barn floor was covered with hay, and there was a hill of hay which led right up to the scaffold; so they could get there well enough without being bewitched."

"Did your mother—my great-grandma—believe in witches?" asked Prudy.

"What did she say to Mr. Palmer?"

"O, no! she had no faith in witches; thy great grandmother was a sensible woman." She said to him, "Friend Asa, thee'd better have some good strong bows made for thy cattle, and put on their necks; and then I think thee'll find they can't get out of their stalls. Thee says they are as lean as Pharaoh's kine, and I would advise thee to feed them better. Cattle that are well fed and well cared for will never go bewitched."

"Did Mrs. Knowles know what people said about her?" asked Prudy.

"Yes; she heard the stories, and it made her feel very badly."

"How did she look?"

"A little like thy grandmother Parlin, if I remember, only she was much larger."

"Did she know anything?"

"O, yes; it was rather an ignorant neighborhood; but she was one of the most intelligent women in it."

"Did she ever go anywhere?"

"Yes; she came to my mother for sympathy. I remember just how she looked in her tow and linen dress, with her hair fastened at the back of the head with a goose-quill."

"There, there!" cried Dotty, "that was what made 'em call her a witch!"

"O, no; a goose-quill was quite a common fashion in those times, and a great deal prettier, too, than the waterfalls thee sees nowadays. Mrs. Knowles dressed like other people, and looked like other people, for aught I know; but I wished she would not come to our house so much."

"Didn't you like her?"

"Yes; I liked her very well, for she carried peppermints in a black bag on her arm; but I was afraid the stories were true, and she might bewitch my mother."

"Why, grandma, I shouldn't have thought that of you!"

"I was a very small girl then, Prudence; and the children I played with belonged, for the most part, to ignorant families."

"Grandma was like an apple playing with potatoes," remarked Dotty, one side to Prudy.

"I used to watch Mrs. Knowles," continued Mrs. Read, "hoping to see her cry; for they said if she was really a witch, she could shed but three tears, and those out of her left eye."

"Did you ever catch her crying?"

"Once," replied grandma, with a smile; "and then she kept her handkerchief at her face. I was quite disappointed, for I couldn't tell which eye she cried out of."

"Please tell some more," said Dotty.

"They said Mrs. Knowles was often seen in a high wind riding off on a broomstick. It ought to have been a strong broomstick, for she was a very large woman."

"Why, grandma," said Prudy, thrusting her hook into a stitch, "I can't help thinking what queer days you lived in! Now, when I talk to my grandchildren, I shall tell them of such beautiful things; of swings and picnics, and Christmas trees."

"So shall I to my grandchildren," said Dotty; "but not always. I shall have to look sober sometimes, and tell 'em how I had the sore throat, and couldn't swallow anything but boiled custards and cream toast. 'For,' says I, 'children, it was very different in those days.'"

"Ah, well, you little folks look forward, and we old folks look backward; but it all seems like a dream, either way, to me," said grandma Read, binding off the thumb of her little red mitten—"like a dream when it is told."

"Speaking of telling dreams, grandma, I had a funny one last night," said

Prudy, "about a queer old gentleman. Guess who it was."

"Thy grandfather, perhaps. Does thee remember, Alice, how thee used to sit on his knee and comb his hair with a toothpick?"

"I don't think 'twas me," said Dotty; "for I wasn't born then."

"It was I," replied Prudy. "I remember grandpa now, but I didn't use to.

It wasn't grandpa I dreamed about—it was Santa Claus."

Grandma smiled, and raised her spectacles to the top of her forehead.

"We never talked about fairies in my day," said she. "I never heard of a

Santa Claus when I was young."

"Well, grandma, he came down the chimney in a coach that looked like a Quaker bonnet on wheels—but he was all a-dazzle with gold buttons; and what do you think he said?"

"Something very foolish, I presume."

"He said, 'Miss Prudy, I'm going to be married.' Only think! and he such a very old bachelor."

"Did thee dream out the bride?"

"It was Mother Goose."

"Very well," said Mrs. Read, smiling. "I should think that was a very good match."

"She did look so funny, grandma, with a great hump on her nose, and one on her back! Santa Claus kissed her; and what do you think she said?"

"I am sure I can't tell; I am not acquainted with thy fairy folks."

"Why, she shook her sides, and, said she, 'Sing a song o' sixpence.'"

"That was as sensible a speech as thee could expect from that quarter."

"O, grandma, you don't care anything about my dream, or I could go on and describe the wedding-cake; how she put sage in it, and pepper, and mustard, and baked it on top of one of our registers. What do you suppose made me dream such a queer thing?"

"Thee was probably thinking of thy mother's wedding."

"O, Christmas is going to be splendided than ever, this year," said Dotty; "isn't it grandma? Did you have any Christmases when you were young?"

"O, yes; but we didn't make much account of Christmas in those days."

"Why, grandma! I knew you lived on bean porridge, but I s'posed you had something to eat Christmas!"

"O, sometimes I had a little saucer-pie, sweetened with molasses, and the crust made of raised dough."

"Poor, dear grandma!"

"I remember my father used to put a great backlog on the fire Christmas morning, as large as the fireplace would hold; and that was all the celebration we ever had."

"Didn't you have Christmas presents?"

"No, Alice; not so much as a brass thimble."

"Poor grandma! I shouldn't think you would have wanted to live! Didn't anybody love you?" said Dotty, putting her fingers under Mrs. Read's cap, and smoothing her soft gray hair; "why, I love every hair of your head."

"I am glad thee does, child; but that doesn't take much love, for thee knows I haven't a great deal of hair."

"But, grandma, how could you live without Christmas trees and things?"

"I was happy enough, Alice."

"But you'd have been a great deal happier, grandma, if you'd had a Santa

Claus! It's so nice to believe what isn't true!"

"Ah! does thee think so? There was one thing I believed when I was a very little girl, and it was not true. I believed the cattle knelt at midnight on Christmas eve."

"Knelt, grandma? For what?"

"Because our blessed Lord was born in a manger."

"But they didn't know that. Cows can't read the Bible."

"It was an idle story, of course, like the one about Mother Knowles. A man who worked at our house, Israel Grossman, told it to me, and I thought it was true."

Here grandma gazed into the coals again. She could see Israel Grossman sitting on a stump, whittling a stick and puffing away at a short pipe.

"Well, children," said she, "I have talked to you long enough about things that are past and gone. On the whole, I don't say they were good old times, for the times now are a great deal better."

"Yes, indeed," said Prudy.

"Except one thing," added grandma, looking at Dotty, who was snapping the tongs together. "Children had more to do in my day than they have now."

Dotty blushed.

"Grandma," said she, "I'm having a playtime, you know, 'cause there can't anybody stop to fix my work. But mother says after the holidays I'm going to have a stint every day."

"That's right, dear. Now thee may run down and get me a skein of red yarn thee will find on the top shelf in the nursery closet."

CHAPTER XI.

THE CRYSTAL WEDDING.

As the crystal wedding was to take place on the twenty-fourth, the Christmas tree was deferred till the night after, and was not looked forward too by the children as anything very important. They had had a tree, a Kris Kringle, or something of the sort, every year since they could remember; but a wedding was a rare event, and to be a bridesmaid was as great an honor, Dotty thought, as could be conferred on any little girl.

It was intended that everything should be as much as possible like the original wedding. Mrs. Parlin was to wear the same dove-colored silk and bridal veil she had worn then, and Mr. Parlin the same coat and white vest, though they were decidedly out of fashion by this time. Dotty was resplendent in a white dress with a long sash, a gold necklace of her aunt Eastman's, and a pair of white kid slippers. Johnny was to be groomsman. He was a boy who was always startling his friends with some new idea, and this time he had "borrowed" a silver bouquet-holder out of his mother's drawer, and filled it with the loveliest greenhouse flowers.

Until Dotty saw this, she had been happy; but the thought of standing up with a boy who held such a beautiful toy, while her own little hands would be empty—this was too much.

"Johnny Eastman," said she, with a trembling voice, "how do you think it will look to be holding flowers up to your nose when the minister's a-praying? I'd be so 'shamed, so 'shamed, Johnny Eastman!"

"You want the bouquet-holder yourself, you know you do," said Johnny; "you want everything you see; and if folks don't give right up to you, then there's a fuss."

"O, Johnny Eastman, I'm a girl, and that's the only reason why I want the bouquet-holder! If I was a boy, do you s'pose I'd touch such a thing? But I can't wear flowers in the button-holes of my coat—now can I?"

The children were in the guest chamber, preparing to go down—all but Prudy, who was in her mother's room, assisting at the bridal toilet. Susy and Flossy stood before the mirror, and Johnny and Dotty in the middle of the room, confronting each other with angry brows.

"Hush, children!" said Susy, in an absentminded way, and went on brushing her hair, which was one of the greatest trials in the whole world, because it would not curl. She had frizzed it with curling-tongs, rolled it on papers, and drenched it with soap suds till there was danger of its fading entirely away; still it was as straight, after all, as an Indian's.

"O, dear!" said she; "it sticks up all over my head like a skein of yarn.

Children, do hush!"

"Mine curls too tight, if anything; don't you think so?" asked Flossy, trying not to look as well satisfied with herself as she really felt; adding, by way of parenthesis, "Johnny, why can't you be quiet?"

"Are you going to let me have that bouquet-holder, Johnny Eastman?" continued Dotty; "'cause I'm going right out to tell my mother. She'll be so mortified she'll send you right home, if you hold it up to your nose, when you are nothing but a boy."

"That's right, Dimple, run and tell."

"No, I shan't tell if you'll give it to me. And you may have one of the roses in your button-hole, Johnny. That's the way the Pickings man had, that wrote Little Nell; father said so. There's a good boy, now!"

Dotty dropped her voice to a milder key, and smiled as sweetly as the bitterness of her feelings would permit. She had set her heart on the toy, and her white slippers, and even her gold necklace, dwindled into nothing in comparison.

"Whose mother owns this bouquet-holder, I'd like to know?" said Johnny, flourishing it above his head. "And whose father brought home the flowers from the green-house?"

"Well, any way, Johnny, 'twas my aunt and uncle, you know; and they'd be willing, 'cause your mamma let me have her necklace 'thout my asking."

"I can't help it if they're both as willing as two peas," cried Johnny.

"I'm not willing myself, and that's enough."

"O, what a boy! I was going to put some of my nightly blue sirreup on your hangerjif, and now I won't—see if I do!"

"I don't want anybody's sirup," retorted Johnny; "'tic'ly such a cross party's as you are."

"Johnny Eastman, you just stop murdering me."

"Murdering you?"

"Yes; 'he that hateth his brother.'"

"I'm not your brother, I should hope."

"Well, a cousin's just as bad."

"No, not half so bad. I wouldn't be your brother if I had to be a beggar."

"And I wouldn't let you be a brother, Johnny Eastman, not if I had to go and be a heathen."

"O, what a Dotty!"

"O, what a Johnny!"

By this time the little bridesmaid's face was anything but pleasant to behold. Both her dimples were buried out of sight, and she had as many wrinkles in her forehead as grandma Head. Johnny danced about the room, holding before her eyes the bone of contention, then drawing it away again in the most provoking manner.

"If you act so, Johnny Eastman, I won't have you for my bridegroom."

"And I won't have you for my bride—so there!"

The moment these words were spoken, the angry children were frightened. They had not intended to go so far. It had been their greatest pleasure for several weeks to think of "standing up" at a wedding; and they would neither of them have missed the honor on any account. But now, in their foolish strife, they had made it impossible to do the very thing they most desired to do. They had said the fatal words, and were both of them too proud to draw back. There was one comfort. "The wedding will be stopped," thought Dotty; "they can't be married 'thout Johnny and me."

The guests were all assembled. It was now time for the bridal train to go down stairs and have the ceremony performed. As the children left the chamber, uncertain what to do, but resolved that whichever "stood up," the other would sit down, Johnny seized a bottle of panacea which stood on the mantel, and wet the corner of Dotty's handkerchief.

"There is some sirup worth having," said he; "stronger than yours. Rub it in your eyes, and see if it isn't."

The boy did not mean what he said, or at any rate we will hope he did not; but Dotty, in her haste and agitation, obeyed him without stopping one moment to think.

Instantly the wedding was forgotten, the bouquet-holder, the anger, the disappointment, and everything else but the agony in her eyes. It was so dreadful that she could only scream, and spin round and round like a top.

A scene of confusion followed. The poor child was so frantic that her father was obliged to hold her by main force, while her mother tried to bathe her eyes with cold water. They were fearfully inflamed, and for a whole hour the wedding was delayed, while poor Dotty lay struggling in her father's arms, or tore about the nursery like a wild creature.

Johnny was very sorry. He said he did not know what was in the bottle; he had sprinkled his cousin's handkerchief in sport.

"She talks so much about her 'nightly blue sirreup,'" said he to his mother, "that I thought I would tease her a little speck."

"I don't know but you have put her eyes out," said his mother, severely.

"O, do you think so?" wailed Johnny. "O, don't say so, mother!"

"I hope not, my child; but panacea is a very powerful thing. I don't know precisely what is in it, but you have certainly tried a dangerous experiment."

"I didn't mean to, mother; I'll never do so again."

"That is what you always say," replied his mother, shaking her head; "and that is why I am so discouraged about you. Nothing seems to make any impression upon you. If you have really made your cousin blind for life I hope it will be a lesson to you."

While Mrs. Eastman talked, looking very stately in her velvet dress, Master Johnny was balancing himself on the hat-tree in the hall, as if he scarcely heard what she said; but, in spite of his disrespectful manner, he was really unhappy.

"I knew something would go wrong," continued Mrs. Eastman, "when it was first proposed that you and Dotty should stand up together, and I did not approve of the plan. What is the reason you two children must always be quarrelling?"

"She is the one that begins it," replied Johnny. "If I could have stood up with Prudy, there wouldn't have been any fuss."

"With Prudy, indeed! I dare say you would be glad to do so now, you naughty boy. Your kind aunt Mary suggested it, but I told her, No. Since you have hurt Dotty so terribly, you cannot be groomsman."

"O, mother!"

"No, my son. She is unable to perform her part, and you must give up yours. Percy will take your place."

In spite of his manliness, Johnny dropped a few tears, which he brushed away with the back of his hand; but his mother, for once in her life, was firm.

I will not say that Johnny's disappointment was not some consolation to Dotty, who lay on the sofa in the parlor with her eyes bandaged, while the wedding ceremony was performed. If Johnny had been one of the group, while her own poor little self was left out, necklace, slippers, and all, she would have thought it unjust.

As it was, it seemed hard enough. She was in total darkness, but her "mind made pictures while her eyes were shut." She could almost see how the bride and bridegroom looked, holding each other by the hand, with the tall Percy on one side, and the short Prudy on the other,—the dear Prudy, who was so sorry for her sister that she could not enjoy taking her place, though a fairer little bridesmaid than she made could hardly be found in the city.

The same clergyman officiated now who had married Mr. and Mrs. Parlin fifteen years before; and after he had married them over again, he made a speech which caused Dotty to cry a little under her handkerchief; or, if not the speech, it was the panacea that brought the tears—she did not know which.

He said he remembered just how Edward Parlin and Mary Read looked when they stood before him in the bloom of their youth, and promised to live together as husband and wife. They had seemed very happy then; but he thought they were happier now; he could read in their faces the history of fifteen beautiful years. He did not wonder the time had passed very pleasantly, for they knew how to make each other happy; they had tried to do right, and they had three lovely children, who were blessings to them, and would be blessings to any parents.

It was here that Dotty felt the tears start.

"I'm not a blessing at all," thought she; "he doesn't know anything about it, how I act, and had temper up stairs with Johnny! Johnny's put my eyes out for it, and I'll have to go to the 'Sylum, I suppose. If I do, I shan't be a blessing so much as I am now! To anybody ever!"

By and by aunt Eastman presented the bride with a bridal rose, which looked as nearly as possible like the one she had given her at the first wedding, and which grew from a slip of the same plant. Dotty could not see the rose, but she heard her aunt say she hoped to attend Mrs. Parlin's Golden Wedding.

"I shall be ever so old by that time," thought the little girl. "Fifteen from fifty leaves—leaves—I don't know what it leaves; but I shall be a blind old lady, and wear a cap. Perhaps God wants to make a very good woman of me, same as Emily, and that's why he let Johnny put my eyes out."

Here some one came along and offered Miss Dimple a slice of wedding cake, which tasted just as delicious as if she could see it; then some one else put a glass of lemonade to her lips.

"Has my little girl a kiss for me?" said Mrs. Parlin, coming to the sofa as soon as she could break away from her guests.

The gentle "mother-touch" went to Dotty's heart. She threw her arms about

Mrs. Parlin's neck, wrinkling her collar and tumbling her veil.

"Take care, my child," said Mr. Parlin, laughing; "do not crush the bride. Everybody has been coming up to salute her, and you must understand that she does you a great honor to go to you and beg a kiss."

"It is just like you, though, mamma. You are so good to me, and so is everybody! No matter how naughty I am, and spoil weddings, they don't say, 'You hateful thing!'"

"Would it make you a better child, do you think, Dotty, to be scolded when you do wrong?"

"Why, no, indeed, mamma. It's all that makes me not be the wickedest girl in this city, is 'cause you are so good to me; I know it is."

Mrs. Parlin kissed the little mouth that said these sweet words.

"And now that I am blind, mamma, you are so kind, I s'pose you'll feed me with a spoon."

"You will surely be taken care of, dear, as long as your eyes are in this state."

"But shan't I be always blind?"

"No, indeed, child; you will be quite well in a day or two."

"O, I'm so glad, mamma. I was thinking I shouldn't ever go to school, and should have to be sent to the 'Sylum."

While Dotty was speaking, Johnny came up to the sofa, and, taking her hand, said, in a tone of real sorrow,—

"Look here, Dotty; I was a naughty boy; will you forgive me?"

As Johnny was not in the habit of begging pardon, and did it now of his own free will, Dotty was greatly astonished.

"Yes, Johnny," said she, "I forgive you all up. But then I don't ever want you to put my eyes out again."

"I won't, now, honest; see 'f I do," replied Master Johnny, in a choked voice. "And you may have that bouquet-holder, to keep; mother said so."

"O, Johnny!"

"Yes; mother says we can call it a 'peace offering.' Let's not quarrel any more, Dotty, just to see how 'twill seem."

"What, never!" exclaimed Dotty, starting up on her elbow, and trying to look through her thick bandage at Johnny. "Never! Why, don't you mean to come to my house any more, Johnny Eastman?"

"Yes; but I won't quarrel unless you begin it."

"O, I shan't begin it," replied Miss Dimple, confidently; "I never do, you know."

Johnny had the grace not to retort. He was ashamed of his ungentlemanly conduct, and knelt before the sofa, gazing sadly at his blindfolded little cousin. It was a humble place for him, and we will leave him there, hoping his penitence may do him good for the future.

As for Miss Dimple, we will bid her goodbye while her eyes are closed. Be patient, little Dotty; the pain will soon be over, and when we see you again, you will be trudging merrily to school with a book under your arm.